SAVING THE PACK

THE WOODLAND WOLF PACKS
BOOK THREE

AMELIA SHAW

TAMSIN BAKER

I was going to be sick, and the toilet was too far away.

I ran as fast as I could, knocking my knee painfully against the bathroom door frame as I rushed into the tiny room. "Ow!"

The heat in my face rose and I grabbed for my hair, holding it out of the way as I launched my body forward.

"Bleh...."

The acidic bile rushed up my throat and into the toilet bowl, splashing against the sides and making me retch and choke even further. The smell burnt my nose and tears rolled down my cheeks, until finally, mercifully, it stopped.

I reached for the thin toilet paper beside me, pulling it from the roll and dabbing at my mouth.

I swallowed hard, though my mouth was too dry.

Yuck.

"Oh... dear God." That was terrible.

And it hadn't stopped yet.

Every day I'd been sick.

Every morning, to be precise. Until about lunchtime.

For two weeks.

I couldn't ignore the truth any longer.

"I'm in trouble here."

The front door to the apartment banged open and I jumped up off the floor and took a seat on the toilet, my head spinning with fatigue and low blood pressure.

"Celeste!"

I pushed the bathroom door quickly shut and pulled down my pants, so it looked like I was using the toilet for something more than vomiting.

In case he came in. Like he had done many times in the past.

There was no such thing as privacy if you were a member of the Little Rock bear's den.

I called out to him. "In the bathroom. I'll be out soon."

The bile rose again. *Oh, no.* My gut churned and tightened.

I closed my eyes and forced the vomit back down, swallowing hard against the automatic reflex to let it all out.

I couldn't let them know my secret.

I couldn't.

They'd never forgive me.

Loud footsteps walked up the hallway, then a fist pounded the door, hard.

I jumped, shivering with fear.

"Hurry up!" The voice was rough and loud. "The kitchen isn't going to clean itself, woman!"

I rolled my eyes, but only because he couldn't see me. If anyone in this place knew the kitchen needed cleaning, it was me.

"Um, one minute. Sorry. I'll be right out."

He grunted and walked away.

I relaxed against the commode as I heard his footsteps fade away, my whole body shaking with stress.

How long was I going to be able to hide this from the den?

And when they finally found out, which was inevitable, what would they do? Force me to get an abortion? Or something worse?

I exhaled in a long sigh. *Time to get moving before he came back and dragged me out.*

I opened the bathroom door and moved to the sink to splash some cold water onto my hot cheeks.

Uncle Dennis, my adoptive father's brother, was my "employer". He had set me up to work seven days a week in a job no one else would do—cleaning this run-down block of apartments.

The bears owned the apartment block. Some of the floors were rented out to outsiders, but the rest were occupied by members of the den, including me.

And the way I paid for my tiny bedroom in this apartment I shared with four others, was to clean every bathroom in the block.

All forty-six of them.

I took a deep breath and exhaled slowly, garnering whatever self-preserving courage I had.

Just one step at a time. You can do this.

I walked to the old kitchen and grabbed some saltine crackers from the cupboard, crunching on the only thing that seemed to keep the nausea at bay.

I took a moment to allow the food to reach my belly and settle the queasiness, and then I got to work.

Of course, it wasn't just my job to clean every bathroom in the block of apartments. It was also my *delight* to clean the kitchen and the entire apartment I slept in. Even though five of us lived here.

I had just finished wiping down the benches and cleaning out the kitchen sink, when my nose began to burn with a sudden foul smell. My throat convulsed. *Oh, no. The others were back.*

Then the front door flew open and three, burly, bear-shifting men walked in.

Great. My uncle was front and center, strolling in with two of the others who'd shunned me when they found out I was human.

The smell of them.... *Oh my God.*

I couldn't hold in the need to throw up, the second their musty stench hit my nostrils.

I rushed to the newly cleaned kitchen sink. My back heaved as my stomach emptied the meager contents I'd managed to keep down.

"What's going on with you? You sick again?" My uncle's voice was angry, annoyed. Like it always was whenever he spoke to me. Or at least, like it had been ever since I reached maturity and the bears had decided I was unworthy of a mate.

Not a single man from the den had wanted me.

Not that I'd wanted any of them, either. But it hurt. Despite all my hopes and dreams of a real family, I'd been rejected.

Wholeheartedly.

I nodded and rinsed out my mouth as quickly as I could. "Ah, yeah... sorry. I'll get back to cleaning."

I kept my head down, attempting to walk around the three man-mountains standing in the middle of the kitchen.

Each smelled as bad as the other.

"Stop."

The command in my uncle's voice made me freeze. Or as close as I could, considering I was shivering like a leaf in the Fall breeze.

"What...?" My uncle bent down and smelled me, sniffing loudly, before his lip curled up in a snarl. "You smell even worse than usual. Almost like a.... wolf."

My eyes closed and my stomach dropped to my feet.

They knew.

They must know, and they would punish me for my mistake.

Rough hands grabbed my chin and forced my head up.

"Open your eyes."

I did as commanded, and Uncle Dennis's eyes bored into mine.

"Tell me. Now."

"What... I mean... Tell you?" I was stammering, I was so scared.

My arms and legs shook. Goosebumps covered my skin.

I felt as if I would fall to the floor if he let go of my jaw.

"Lou, Davie, come here and smell her. Tell me if you smell what I do?"

Oh, God, no!

I kept my arms pinned to my sides and tried not to breathe.

This was the most humiliating thing about being part of this family. They all said I smelled weird.

Worse than weird. Bad. Disgusting.

Or that's what the bears said.

So, I scrubbed myself clean three times a day, even taking antiseptic into the shower some days to disinfect myself.

It hadn't changed anything.

They still hated me and said my smell made them sick.

"She's knocked up," Lou grunted.

"Yeah, but by who?" Uncle Dennis growled.

He shifted his grip to my throat and forced me backward until my spine touched the wall. I gasped for air, trying to control my growing panic.

No!

I grabbed for his hands and pulled on them, trying to loosen his grip, the pain making my head spin. He squeezed tighter, until I couldn't breathe at all.

Oh God... Am I going to choke to death, right here, at his hand?

"None of us wanted you, so it can't be a bear's baby. Who was it, you little slut?"

I couldn't lie. I had to tell them the truth. I'd been lonely and desperate, and the man I'd met made me feel more loved in a single hour than I'd ever experienced my whole life.

He released me enough that I could finally answer him.

"Just... a guy. In town. At a bar."

Uncle Dennis dropped me to the ground. I inhaled quickly, needing the air. I stayed where I was, on my hands and knees.

I wasn't getting back up just to be knocked down again. I'd learnt that lesson the hardest way, many times over.

As one of the only non-shifting women in the whole den, I was the weakest by far. I had the scars and the healed broken bones to prove it.

"It smells like a wolf," he growled above me.

I kept my head down. They weren't talking to me.

"We always knew she smelled like them," Uncle Dennis said.

"One of their human mates." Lou spat.

What?

I listened intently, though I tried not to show how interested I was.

A wolf's fated mate? How was that possible? I knew about the concept of fated mates, of course. I'd lived among the bear shifters for long enough. But... I was human. That seemed impossible, in my mind.

"You know the Alpha doesn't want the wolves getting any more of them," Lou growled and I heard Uncle Dennis's sigh.

Any more of them? Of what? Humans? Mates? What are they talking about?

"Let's take her to the Alpha and find out what he wants to do with her."

They hoisted me to my feet, and I went with them without complaint, even though the Alpha, Trevor, terrified me even more than Uncle Dennis. Being submissive to the bears had kept me alive and relatively well fed.

I relaxed as much as I could, calm descending over me. It was probably unnatural and unhealthy, this calmness, but I'd known this day would come, sooner or later.

They'd realize I wasn't suited for their den, and they'd either kick me out, or ship me off somewhere.

But now that the worst had finally arrived, my shakes and panic seemed to disappear. My mind worked faster than it ever had, focusing in on the one thought that mattered. There was more than me at stake now. My baby needed protection from the men who towered over us.

There was only one thing to do. As soon as I got the chance, I had to run.

And thanks to Lou inadvertently spilling the beans about my wolf-like smell, I now knew where to go for refuge.

Tayte, the Alpha wolf-shifter from the bar, had said something strange the night we met.

About a woman, a doctor, who was the first human mate they'd found in town.

I'd memorized that piece of information somehow through my alcohol-fogged brain.

My baby and I needed protection, and the daddy wolf who had made this baby with me was the only one who could give us the protection we needed.

DEATH!

They'd sentenced me to death!

The family that had taken me in as a baby, and raised me. The family I'd slaved for, all these years. Whom I'd tried to love to the best of my ability. I'd spent years caring for their children, their homes... and this was the result?

With a single word from the new Alpha, Trevor, they decided I needed to die.

I still couldn't believe it.

They'd all turned their backs on me.

I sat in my locked bedroom, still stunned at the turn of events. They had chosen to kill me in the morning, because tonight they were too busy with important bear pack stuff to bother with a little human like me.

They probably thought I'd never even consider escape. But they were wrong.

So wrong.

I placed my hands gently over my stomach. I had the incentive now, and I wouldn't sit around and wait to be killed, like they probably assumed I'd do.

Idiots. They hadn't even bothered to chain me up.

In the past I'd always meekly fallen in with their plans.

Not this time.

Not when my life, and that of my growing baby, was on the line.

As soon as the noise of the pack quietened down halfway through the night, indicating that most, if not all of them were finally asleep, I managed to pick the lock and break out of my bedroom. I'd done it before, when they'd left me alone, in case I ever needed to get away one day. Not that I thought I'd ever actually need the skill. But it wasn't difficult with the old locks, and a couple of hair pins bent in a particular way.

I crept through the apartment, avoiding the creaking wood panels I knew by heart, and ran. Through the exit door into the stairwell, down the many flights of stairs and out into the cold night air.

I didn't even stop to shiver in the tank top and thin jeans I wore. I just started running. Through the city, heading for the hospital. Toward the woman who might be able to help me.

A doctor, named Claire.

God... please.

The bear's apartment block was as far away from the inner city as they could get, almost on the outskirts of the city, in fact, but the streetlights lit my path, showing me the way to safety.

My heart galloped in my chest.

My throat burned as I gasped air in and out of my lungs.

And I didn't stop.

As soon as the bears realized I was gone, they would chase me, and I'd be done for. I had no protection, no weapon. The only things I had were my two legs and the will of a mother fighting for her child's life.

It had to be enough.

I kept running, city block after city block, though my tired body screamed at me to stop.

Adrenaline pumped harder through my system and I increased my pace, turning corners as quickly as I could.

The streets were deserted. It had to be past two a.m.

I didn't really know the exact time.

I kept going, pausing to breathe at an intersection to get my bearings, my chest heaving with exertion.

Which way?

They didn't let me out into the city very much and I wasn't familiar with the street signs, though I'd lived here all my life.

I looked and looked, then saw a sign I recognized.

Yes! The supermarket. It isn't far from the hospital.

Keep going.

I pushed off again, my legs screaming at me for those first few steps until I found my rhythm once more.

The hospital, safety, was about six blocks now, by my reckoning. My thigh muscles burned as I tripped on some uneven pavement, but I kept running.

The night was silent, except for my ragged breathing.

I could only imagine what would happen when the bears

woke to find me gone. Growling and screams of rage would follow. I knew their tempers, their fighting and hunting abilities.

I'd watched them my whole life. And if I became the hunted, rather than the observer, then I was as good as dead.

Unless I could find her in time.

Claire. The doctor.

I turned one more corner and ground to a halt.

There it was.

A huge, white building with bright lights and doors that opened automatically.

I staggered the last hundred feet, my energy depleted and my body relaxing as my safe haven was finally in sight.

I stopped on the sidewalk, fear skittling through me.

The bears would be able to track me straight here if I went inside the hospital right now. They'd already tracked Claire there once.

I had to throw them off the scent, at least a little.

Damn it.

I staggered to the right, going another block down, though fear truly raced along my nerves now.

I ripped off my tank and dropped it onto a park bench.

I walked to the next bench and took off my jeans, leaving them beneath the seat.

"Oh my God." It was freaking freezing!

I jumped up and down, clad only in my old underwear, and then ran back to the hospital.

Hopefully that would help.

I ran straight into the Emergency Room and the bright lights enveloped me.

I was shaking, freezing, panting and half-naked. I felt as if I were about to drop to the floor in a faint.

Nurses rushed at me from everywhere, with blankets and juice, and nice words.

They admitted me straight away.

"What's happened dear, were you attacked? Shall we call the police?"

An old nurse was preparing a bag of fluid and as she came for me, needle ready to put in my arm. I stopped her.

"Can I please have a shower? I smell bad, and I'm so cold."

My scent would be greatly reduced after a shower. And thanks to the bears grabbing me early yesterday and then locking me up, I hadn't had one in over twenty-four hours.

"Of course, you can, after we've done a few tests."

I stood up. I couldn't let her win this one. "No please. It's important. I'm pregnant and I need to see Claire."

"Claire?" The nurse blinked and put down the needle. "She's not working tonight but I may have someone else who could help you."

I shuffled toward the shower room. "Please. I just need two minutes in the shower, then you can test me as much as you like."

The nurse nodded and I jumped into the shower, scrubbing my trembling body with the sterile-smelling soap and even washing my hair. Someone had left some shampoo in the stall and I couldn't resist. I didn't get that luxury much at home.

"Here you go." Someone stuck her arm into the cubicle and offered me a fresh white towel.

I turned off the water and reached for the towel. It was clean and fluffy. "Oh, that's heavenly! Thank you."

The person behind the door laughed.

"What's funny?" I asked, frowning her way, though she couldn't see me.

Surely the fact that a hospital towel was the cleanest piece of linen I'd seen in my whole life wasn't to be laughed at.

"I'll explain in a sec. I was told you came in with no clothes. I had some spare yoga pants and a sweater in my locker."

She placed the bag just inside the bathroom, then shut the door again.

Tears prickled in my eyes and I blinked them back.

"That's... ah ... so kind of you."

I quickly dried my body and wrapped my wet hair with the towel.

The yoga pants were the perfect size, though a little tight around my tummy, and the jumper was snuggly and warm, though way too big.

How tall was this woman?

I glanced at my reflection in the mirror. I was red and blotchy, but clean and safe.

I'd take it.

When I stepped out of the bathroom there was a young nurse sitting on the bed.

She grinned at me with a lazy confidence I'd only seen in the extremely powerful shifters in my den.

All men.

"Um... I'm Celeste," I said.

She grinned. "Nevaeh."

"Nevaeh..." I'd never heard that name before.

"That's why I laughed. You said, heavenly. My name is heaven spelled backwards."

I stared at her, wondering if she was joking.

She laughed. "It's true. Hippie parents. I used to hate it, but since meeting my guys, I don't stress anymore."

Had she just said "guys"? As in, more than one?

She didn't answer my question, though. Instead, she pulled her cell phone from her pocket.

"I know you wanted to see Claire, but she's at home. She's pregnant and working less hours. Why did you ask for her?" Nevaeh's tone was casual, but I had the strangest feeling she knew why I was here.

"Ah... that's great about her being pregnant."

Maybe I shouldn't have come here? I didn't know these people. How could I trust them?

This was a stupid idea.

I edged toward the door.

"Um... I think I'll get going."

Nevaeh stood up. "Hey, don't freak out. You're pregnant, too?"

I hesitated, then realized I'd told the first nurse the truth. So, I nodded.

Nevaeh moved around the room and gestured to the bed. "I'm not going to hurt you, I promise. Have a seat and I'll explain."

I had pretty good instincts when it came to evil intent, and as I reached out with those senses, I came up with nothing.

Hmmm... okay.

I walked back to the small bed, climbed onto the thin mattress and pulled the blanket over me. It was so nice to be warm.

Nevaeh stepped toward me, her movements slow and nonthreatening. "Mind if I put the drip in now that you've showered?"

I nodded. "Sure."

Not for me, but for the baby.

I rolled up my sleeve and she walked the rest of the way across to me, sliding the needle into my hand effortlessly and then taping it down.

Wow. She was good at that.

"You need your fluids," she said, as though that explained everything, then sat again in the chair by the bed. "Look, Celeste, I'm willing to tell you everything about me and Claire, but you have to *show* me that you need to know. If you know what I mean?"

She smiled and waited. I got the drift and sighed.

What did I have to lose at this point?

"I've lived with the bear shifters just near the edge of town, for most of my life. But they found out yesterday that I'm pregnant and they decided to kill me. Me and my baby. So, I ran."

Nevaeh slid to the edge of her chair. "Holy shit."

"Yeah."

Then she snorted. "Sounds like my last month."

Sorry? "Ah... what?"

Nevaeh shrugged and met my gaze. "I'm not sure if you heard what happened with Trevor and his dad, but I'm the female that Trevor was stalking."

She was the girl? My gaze ran over the woman in front of me. Tall, thin and super-pretty. "You're the one who killed our Alpha."

I was shocked. I'd expected someone so much bigger, stronger, and more shifter-like.

Nevaeh nodded. "Unfortunately, yes that's me. He was trying to kill my mates."

She looked a bit regretful, but not overly sorry. And I didn't blame her, if what she said was true.

"Trevor's our Alpha now. I never much liked his father but Trevor's just as bad. Worse in some ways."

Then I slammed a hand over my mouth. I couldn't believe I'd actually said that!

Such a comment would have normally gotten me whipped, or my arms broken.

Nevaeh winced. "I wish I'd gotten him, too. *Bastard.*" Then her gaze zeroed in on me.

"So, why are you here, Celeste? You obviously know about the shifting world. And you're running from the bears. How can Claire and I help you? And how did you know to come here for her, anyway?"

I licked my dry lips and Nevaeh handed me a bottle of water.

I smiled with gratitude.

She was being so nice to me. I needed to be honest with her. "I heard about Claire from Tayte, a guy I met in a bar a couple of months ago. He told me about his town, and how Claire was the first female mate they'd found in years."

Nevaeh's eyes opened even wider.

"Tayte told you about the pack? About Claire?"

She looked surprised, and a bit upset.

I jumped in to defend him. They probably weren't allowed to tell humans about their world. "Yeah. He could smell the bears on me, so he knew I lived with them. And he was pretty drunk... so was I. I'm not sure he meant to tell me so much, but don't worry, I never said anything to any of the bears about Claire.

They knew anyway, somehow. That the wolves had found their first mate. That's why they tried to keep you away. Wait a minute."

All the pieces suddenly clicked into place. "You're a wolf mate, too!"

Her lips stretched up into a huge smile. "Yes, I am. But do you mean too, as in like Claire... or do you mean too... as in, like *you*?"

She raised her eyebrows and my hands flew to my still-flat stomach.

I didn't want to answer that, and if I were being honest, I didn't really know the answer. I was going only on the word of the bears. What would they know about wolf fated mates?

"Is Tayte the father?" Nevaeh asked quietly.

I waited a heartbeat, then told the truth.

I nodded. "Yes, that's why I came here. To find Claire. To ask for her help in getting to the pack. I know I come with a whole lot of trouble at my back, but I need to find Tayte and see if he will be willing to protect me and the baby."

Nevaeh pulled her cell phone from a pocket and began pressing buttons.

"Who are you calling? It's probably three in the morning."

"Three thirty, actually." Nevaeh put the phone to her ear and gestured for me not to stress with a flutter of her hands. "Trust me, Grayson's gonna wanna hear this."

CHAPTER

TWO

TAYTE

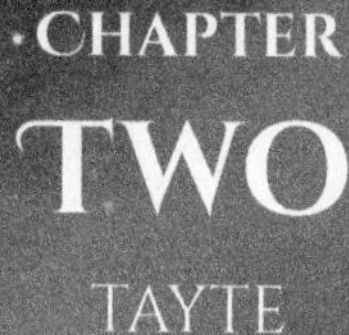

I woke so abruptly from a sound sleep it was like someone had physically thrown me out of my warm bed. "What the…?"

Someone was banging on my front door, and they weren't stopping any time soon.

My eyes sprung open and I jumped out of bed.

"Tayte. What's going on?" My Beta, Sam, yelled from the back of the house as I jogged down the stairs.

"No idea," I called back up.

We never had this sort of drama in the middle of the night.

It was still dark out. Like, pitch black dark.

I turned on a light in the lounge and opened the door, my eyes blinking rapidly to adjust to the artificial brightness.

"Morning," Grayson said, stepping inside without an invitation.

Unusual for an Alpha.

We didn't invade each other's houses like this. It wasn't respectful.

"Still night," I mumbled, rubbing my eyes clear of sleep. "But come on in, Gray." Then I chuckled. "Oh, that's right, you're already in. What the hell is going on?"

Grayson grinned at me. "Put your coffee pot on, Tayte. You're gonna have a visitor soon. You and your pack need to wake up."

Despite my confusion, I stumbled to the kitchen and put the kettle on like he suggested.

Grayson was one of the few selfless Alphas in our larger pack of wolf shifters. If there was anyone I trusted beyond myself to care for my Beta and Omega, it was Gray.

"What's going on?" Sam asked as he practically fell down the stairs. He slept like the dead, that one.

Dane, my Omega, walked downstairs more slowly, already pulling a tank over his bare chest.

I only wore the trackies I slept in, and didn't see any need to dress further.

The Omegas were always more self-conscious than us Alphas.

"Hey, guys," Grayson greeted them, too cheery for this early in the morning.

"You going to tell us why you're here, Gray? Something wrong?"

Grayson had found his mate last month and gone through hell to get her away from a bear shifter.

His next-door neighbor, Dexter, had been the first to find a human mate in the pack.

I didn't know Dex's pack well, but to say I was jealous of their newfound happiness would be an understatement.

"Nothing's wrong. I got a call from Nevaeh at the hospital. Seems a woman staggered into Emergency last night, looking for Claire."

The hairs on my neck prickled up.

Ever since that night two months ago when I'd told a stranger about Claire, I'd been worried something like this might come up.

"Is Claire okay?"

"Yeah, she wasn't working tonight. So, Nevaeh looked after the girl, and she's bringing her home now."

Huh? Nevaeh was bringing another human female here, to the pack. Why? And why was it worth waking us in the middle of the night to communicate that odd piece of news?

Sam and Dane stared at me, clearly confused.

Then the pieces of the puzzle began to fall into place for me.

"This girl... blonde, blue eyes, about five feet tall?"

She had been tiny, and sweet, and very sexy, if my drunken brain hadn't exaggerated the details of that one-night-stand.

"Not sure. I haven't met her yet. But she asked for Claire by name at the hospital and she told Nevaeh that you were the one who told her about Claire."

Grayson gave me a hard look and if I'd been inclined to blush, I would have.

Instead, I thrust my hands into my track pant pockets and shrugged.

"Yeah, I did. And I'm sorry about that. I was drunk, and she already knew about the shifting world. It just kinda slipped out. Seemed natural to tell her, actually, in a weird way."

Sam looked from Gray to me. "So, what are you here to say? Is Tayte in trouble?"

Grayson turned to Sam. "Have you two met her? The girl Tayte slept with a couple of months ago?"

My eyebrows flew up, surprised by Grayson's swift change of topic.

Dane shook his head.

Sam said, "No. He mentioned it. But that night we were working late. Tayte went into town with another pack."

I frowned, trying to remember the details of the evening. I couldn't believe I'd had so much to drink. Why hadn't I waited for my own pack to join me for the trip? That was usually the way we did things.

"Oh, yeah, that's right," I said, as memories started to come back to me. "It wasn't even my night to go into town, but with the news of Claire, I wanted to get in there and at least start looking."

Grayson glanced at his cell phone. "Well, you may have met your destiny that night, Tayte. Looks like she's almost here."

Grayson stood up and went to move past me toward the front door.

I stopped him by grabbing his arm. "What do you mean? Are you telling me she's my fated mate? That's impossible."

There hadn't been any of the signs. No fainting, no intensely sweet smell— though I'd been drunk off my ass—not to mention the fact she smelled of bears.

"Grab a coffee, guys, and then make your way over to our place, all three of you."

Grayson shrugged out of my grasp, gave us a grin then headed out the door.

Dane turned to look at me. "Do you think it's possible, Tayte?"

"I... ah, don't really know."

And I didn't.

Sam crossed his arms over his chest. "And if she's your mate, does that mean she's ours as well? Like with Grayson and Dexter?"

I grabbed our travel mugs and Dane brushed me away, taking over the coffee preparations.

"Thanks."

He did coffee-making better than me.

"Well, we better get dressed, I suppose." I glanced down at my half-naked body. I wasn't sure how Nevaeh would feel if we turned up like this.

"Yep. See you back here in five." Sam jogged back up the stairs.

I was slower. My brain still hadn't quite woken up yet.

Gray hadn't waited for the sun to rise to share this information, which must mean he was excited by the news.

But why?

Was he so interested in building the pack that he was going to foster off a one-night-stand to me and my pack in lieu of the real thing?

A wave of sadness hit me.

I wanted so much more than that.

I craved my fated mate. A woman to complete our small pack. Someone to come home to. To love and cherish. I was old-fashioned that way.

And being born in this era, where there were no wolf-born women, was both frustrating and depressing.

I pulled on jeans, a long-sleeved shirt and some nice shoes.

May as well dress up a little for the meeting.

I trotted back downstairs and the guys were waiting by the front door, coffees in hand.

"Here," Dane said, handing mine over.

It was hot to the touch and warmed my hands nicely.

"What's wrong, Tayte?" Sam asked as we closed the door and began the walk toward Grayson's place.

His pack's house was on the other side of the central shops.

"Just worried I'm about to be disappointed."

There was a beat of silence around us as my words settled with my pack.

"What's she like? Do you remember?" Sam asked suddenly.

"Um…" What *did* I remember? I'd tried so hard to suppress any thoughts of women of late. It was too painful to be reminded of our loneliness all the time. "I remember feelings, more than anything else. She was sweet, and as drunk as I was." I shook my head. "I didn't want to leave her, but she took off straight after we had sex, and the other pack dragged me home. I remember feeling the need to go look for her but being talked out of it. Seriously… I don't have much."

I shook my head and swallowed my coffee, trying to settle the strange feelings shivering through me.

I was nervous and tense.

I stretched my neck from side to side and heard satisfying clicks and pops.

We walked up the street and stepped onto the sidewalk in front of Grayson's house.

The lights were on, the house lit up like a Christmas tree.

But there was darkness all around.

"Do you smell that?" Sam said, lifting his nose to the air.

I did. There was a faint… sweet…

"Oh. My. God."

It was her.

The three of us raced for the front door, opening it and barreling into the house like a bunch of eager puppies.

I righted myself quickly while Sam and Dane took their time, their reflexes not as sharp as mine.

Her smell hit me like a cloud of perfume. Instant, hot and perfect.

My gaze met hers and all the memories came flooding back.

Of her lips against mine.

The softness of her body beneath my hands.

The tiny gasp of pain as I took her for the first time.

"You were a virgin."

Her eyes widened even further. Oh damn...

"Fuck. Sorry—I didn't mean to say that aloud."

She had been, though. Looking back, I should have known before that point. Her reactions had been too innocent, her enthusiasm too real. The pain in that first thrust, too true.

There was an elbow in my side, as Dane and Sam waited to pounce.

"Oh, um... Dane and Sam, this is... Celeste."

Her name rolled off my tongue like it had always been there.

Great save, memory.

Celeste stood up and walked toward me, the oversized clothes not suiting her.

"It's you."

She reached up to touch my face like *I* was the dream, not her. I leaned into her caress, wanting to feel her skin against mine.

She was so tiny, I'd forgotten just how fragile and delicate her tiny frame had been. She cupped my jaw and I turned my face to kiss her smooth palm.

The gasp that ricocheted through the room deafened me.

She began to crumple. I swooped down to scoop her up before she hit the floor, and I began to shake as pleasure pulsed through every vein and muscle at the feel of her beautiful body in my arms.

I heard a female voice in the background, behind the rushing of blood in my ears. "Sam, Dane, touch her as well. Get it all over and done with in one go."

I didn't understand what the woman meant and bared my teeth to my pack as my Omega and Beta rushed forward to put their hands on my mate.

She cried out as if half-waking up, violently arching her back and shivering all over. Then she passed out fully again.

I glared at Dane, then Sam, fighting my wolf to stay down, and they backed away.

Grayson stepped closer and I snarled at the other Alpha.

He needed to stay away from my mate, or so help me God...

Then Nevaeh was there, pushing Gray back, away from me and my mate, and slowly stepping toward me.

"It's okay, Tayte. You've got her, she's safe now. I brought her home from the hospital for you. No one's going to take her away, now. It's all right."

Her words made sense. I knew that somehow, on a rational level, but I couldn't seem to interpret them properly.

My wolf was crawling up my back. Exploding through my humanity. Fighting to get out and take over.

Protect. I had to protect my mate.

Fuck... no!

I couldn't control the shift. Horror slammed into me. I was going to hurt Celeste because I couldn't contain my wolf.

I yelled at my Beta. "Take her, Sam. Quick."

He rushed over and even though I'd called him, demanded his help, a possessive growl erupted out of my throat.

Somehow I found the strength to release Celeste to Sam, and then I backed up to the front door and managed to wrench it open moments before my wolf ripped through me. Muscles transformed, fur sprouting through my skin as my clothes shredded and fell to the ground beside me.

I shook myself as the transformation completed. I looked around the room through my wolf eyes, everything in black and white and gray.

My mate was here, safe in Sam's arms. Safe with my pack.

Though Gray was still there, across the room.

My lip curled up as I glared at him. I didn't want to leave another Alpha alone with my mate. Not when Celeste and I were still unmated.

But I couldn't stay here. I had too much energy to burn off.

Grayson met my gaze calmly, nodding after a moment as though he understood. "I'll come with you." He walked toward me, stripped off his shirt and jeans and his shifter emerged.

The silver wolf matched me in color and size.

An Alpha.

He nudged me in the shoulder with his head and we took off together, running through the woods. Running away from my destiny at this point. So that I could return, clear headed and stronger than ever, and accept whatever path my destiny led me down.

THREE

SAM

I stared down at the beautiful, tiny woman in my arms. My mate. And yet, Ihad no idea what to do with her. I certainly didn't want to put her down.

"You can lay her on our spare bed, if you want?" Nevaeh suggested, gesturing to the fourth bedroom in their house.

I shook my head, feeling stubborn. "Ah, no, I'd rather hold her for a minute."

Nevaeh smiled gently. "Sure, but how 'bout you guys sit down at least. I'll put some breakfast on."

Brad laughed and patted Nevaeh on the back. "She means, *I'll* put some breakfast on. The woman burns toast on a daily basis."

Nevaeh shrugged good-naturedly. "Told you when we mated that I couldn't cook."

Aaron, Nevaeh's other mate, stepped up and kissed her lips possessively, then pulled away with a grin. "Yep. We don't love you for your cooking."

Nevaeh blushed prettily and I began to relax.

She was right. We needed food and time to wait for our mate to wake up.

I found my way to an armchair and sat, pulling Celeste closer into my body and arranging her head on my chest.

I loved the sensations that ran through me, while I held her. While her scent rose up and tickled my nostrils. While tendrils of her hair fell across my bare arms.

"So, ah, what do we do about this, then?" I asked, and everyone else in the room laughed.

Everyone except Dane, that is.

He had his gaze firmly fixed on Celeste, and he pulled up a chair next to me, obviously not wanting to be too far away from the diminutive female.

Aaron and Nevaeh jumped onto the couch together and Brad went to the kitchen to make whatever he was going to make.

None of us liked to cook in our individual pack, so I was hopeful our mate had a little more skill than Nevaeh seemed to have in the kitchen.

But if she didn't—who cared, really? We'd managed okay so far, and take-out existed for a reason.

"No, like seriously. I have questions," I said, repeating my earlier query. "What do we do now? And how do we know if she's just Tayte's mate, or ours as well?"

I brushed her long blonde hair off her face and stared down at her. Even though her eyes were closed, she was beautiful. But she seemed very young.

"And how old is she?"

She barely looked legal. But surely Tayte wouldn't be stupid enough to have taken her if she were underage?

My stomach tightened at the thought.

Tayte had already had her. Been inside her.

My wolf growled and I tightened my hold on her.

"Relax," Aaron said from the couch. "I know you're feeling all sorts of weird, possessive, jealous crap, but it'll pass. Just, you know, focus on something else."

I glared at the other Beta. "You mean I should forget that my Alpha's already had her?"

Aaron nodded. "Yeah, definitely. Because when she wakes, you'll all have her, and she'll love all of you. Have faith in the system, my friend."

I grunted, not able to find the words to tell him to *get fucked* in an eloquent manner.

The anger in me began to rise. Soon it would reach boiling point.

I had to get a grip on myself. I took a few slow breaths, but it didn't help much.

Didn't they understand how frustrating this was?

"You might want to put her down now," Aaron said, and this time I heard the demand in his tone.

I forced myself to breathe deepeer, to think.

Aaron was right. I was only getting worse the longer I sat here with her draped across my lap.

Brad called from the kitchen. "Through that door, Sam. The bed's good to go."

I followed his directions and placed her down on the large bed in their spare room.

Dane was right behind me, staring down at her. "She looks like an angel."

I nodded. "Yeah, she does."

Her golden hair spread over the duvet and encircled her face like a halo.

I turned and walked away, unsettled by the way she made me feel. Angry, possessive, and worried.

When I got back to my seat, my wolf finally began to relax, to settle. I could breathe again. Though tension still held me in its grip, the anger dissipated.

"Told you," Aaron grunted and I nodded at him. Yeah, he'd been right.

"Thanks."

"No problem," he said. "Don't forget, we've been where you are, man."

Brad stepped into the room then, and placed food in front of us on the low coffee table.

Pancakes. Sliced fruit. Cream.

"Wow." The Omega had said he could cook. He clearly wasn't kidding.

"Eat as much as you want," Brad said as he put down a bunch of plates. We all served ourselves, the distraction of food helping with the strange mood that had gripped me.

I piled my plate up as Brad went back to the kitchen to make more.

I looked at Nevaeh, the one who'd brought us our mate.

"What happened tonight at the hospital?"

She picked up a strawberry, dipped it in the cream then ate it before she answered.

"It was a bit crazy, actually. I was just finishing my night shift and one of the nurses came in to say that there was a woman in the ER. She had stumbled in dressed only in her underwear, freezing cold and asking for Claire."

She had been... what?

I stared at Nevaeh. "What do you mean? She was running around town, in the middle of the night, in her underwear?"

Had Fate sent us some sort of cuckoo?

Nevaeh shrugged. "I went straight to her and she was already in the shower, scrubbing herself clean. That behavior, combined with the fact that she said she used to live with a pack of bear shifters, made me think she probably took off her clothes to knock them off the scent. She's young and pretty timid, but there's no doubting she's smart."

Pride blossomed in my heart at the same time as panic whistled through me.

"She was living with the bears? How is that possible?"

Nevaeh shrugged, seemingly unworried by this turn of events.

"I didn't ask her. But seeing as Trevor deliberately dated me, then stalked me for years to keep me from finding you guys, maybe they did the same thing with her? Maybe they smelled the wolf mate scent on her, the same way Trevor smelled it on me."

Dane gasped beside me. "And she somehow escaped them? A whole bear pack? And went straight for Claire. Pretty amazing for anyone to achieve that, let alone someone young and timid, like you say."

Nevaeh began picking at her pancake, eating small pieces of it with her fingers.

"I agree. Though, given she was drinking in the pub the night she met Tayte, its likely she'd be at least twenty-one, I think."

Well, that's comforting.

Dane sat forward on his chair. "And how do we know if she's our mate, too?"

Aaron answered that one. "Did she smell super-sweet to both of you? Like, intoxicating?"

I looked at Dane. "Yeah," we both answered in unison.

"She shook and gasped when you guys touched her, even after she'd touched the Alpha," Nevaeh said.

"Yeah. So?" I said.

Nevaeh grinned. "That's another sign she's your intended mate. It looks like you guys are very much designed to have one mate for your triad. Like us."

Stark relief, unlike anything I'd ever felt, raced through me. Tayte wouldn't leave us for Celeste, and she wouldn't leave us for him. Dane and I wouldn't be left alone, without an Alpha or a mate. "That's... great."

The front door banged open and I looked up.

The sky outside was decorated with red and orange hues now.

A perfect sunrise.

Grayson and Tayte paced back into the room, still in wolf form.

Grayson shook his pelt and stood up, rising from his silver wolf into his massive human form.

He grabbed his clothes from where he'd left them and pulled them back on.

I glanced across to Nevaeh and watched her devour him with her eyes.

Hopefully my mate would look at me like that someday.

When Grayson was dressed, he stared down at Tayte, who hadn't yet turned back.

"What's wrong?"

Tayte looked toward Nevaeh, then his clothes, which had been shredded by the force of his abrupt change.

"Oh, right. Yeah, hang on."

Grayson trotted up the stairs and came back a few minutes later with a pair of jeans and a sweater.

I almost laughed. Tayte was embarrassed to be naked in the room with Nevaeh, but earlier he'd shredded his clothes like a teenager, changing without even thinking about afterward.

"Here." Grayson laid the clothes on the back of the couch and Tayte raced over to the other Alpha, let go of his wolf, and stood up.

He was naked once again in the room.

I tried to distract Nevaeh as Gray's expression hardened and the tension in the room increased.

Alphas were territorial and this situation was uncomfortable for everyone.

"Um... anything else you want to tell us, Nevaeh? About our mate?"

Nevaeh grabbed another strawberry and bit into it.

"She's tough. I can tell you that. I saw a few scars on her, no doubt from injuries she's sustained over the years. Trevor is violent, and I'm guessing many of the other bears in that pack are, too. She may look fragile and innocent, but she'll have some strength to her."

Tayte, now dressed, walked over to where Dane and I sat, and stood behind us.

"That's good to hear," he said. "I hoped Fate wouldn't send us a mate who couldn't cope with our world."

"Oh, she can cope, all right. Those bears are rugged creatures." Nevaeh shuddered. "If she lived with them her whole life, as a human, then she's tougher than any of us realize."

I could feel that Nevaeh was leaving something out.

I stared at her, narrowing my eyes, and she glanced around the room as though avoiding my gaze.

"There's something else, isn't there, Nevaeh? Something you're not telling us."

She looked at Tayte and back to me and Dane, before nodding. "There is something else. But I can't tell you."

"Why not?"

She smiled gently. "Because Celeste will tell you."

There was movement behind Grayson, where he sat on the couch.

It was her... it was Celeste. She was up again!

Dane and I jumped to our feet, and Tayte released a low rumble and crossed his arms over his chest. It seemed that none of us could still when Celeste was in the room.

She walked out into the lounge, her beautiful blue eyes shining at us with a mixture of fear and hope.

She didn't seem afraid of us, though. Whatever she was fearful of, it wasn't a bunch of wolf shifter possible mates.

She just came straight over to us, looking from Tayte, to me to Dane and back again.

"Did I pass out?" she asked, in a voice that sent ripples of awareness over my skin.

She was so beautiful, I couldn't believe it. Soft skin, shiny hair, big, blue eyes.

"Yes. Though your recovery was pretty quick compared to Nevaeh," Grayson answered.

Celeste put her hands into her pockets and glanced back at the other pack's Alpha.

"That's probably because I'd met Tayte before."

"God, you're beautiful," I said without thinking, and she turned her head and smiled brightly up at me.

"What's Nevaeh talking about, Celeste? Is there something we need to know?" Tayte asked.

She nodded. "There's lots of things. Like my background, the bears, everything. But I think..." She turned around to look at Nevaeh, "I think she meant one specific thing. It's the main reason I'm here."

We waited, the air around us completely still with expectation.

You would have heard the proverbial pin drop.

"And that is?" I prompted, dying of the suspense.

She lifted her gaze to meet Tayte's. "I'm pregnant."

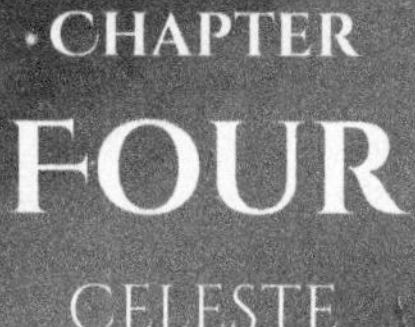

As soon as I said it—my secret, my truth—I heard the swift intake of breath from three shocked shifters.

I wanted to laugh at them.

Was it really so difficult to believe that after a one-night-stand there'd be consequences to our actions?

My hands went reflexively to my flat stomach, which wouldn't be flat for much longer.

I was over eight weeks along now, and Nevaeh had said that wolf shifter pregnancies were slightly different than normal human ones. I'd be bigger, and I'd likely show quicker.

My gaze was still connected with Tayte's, and because of that, I think, the other two men backed away.

To give us room, perhaps? I wasn't sure, but the further away they went, the more the tension in the room seemed to rise.

Tayte, on the other hand, stepped closer. "Are you certain?"

Are you certain it's mine? That was what he was really asking, and I glared up at him. The guy was a foot and a half taller than me, so I had to crane my neck.

"Considering you're the only man I've ever slept with and I'm eight weeks pregnant, vomiting and freaking out, then, yeah, I'm certain."

Part of me marveled at the way I was speaking to an Alpha, and the other part of me cringed a little, wondering if I would be punished for such forward, transgressive behavior.

Uncle Dennis would have back-handed me into the opposite wall if I'd ever tried to speak to him that way.

Tayte was so big and strong and clearly an Alpha leader. Usually, a man like that would terrify me. But even on the night we met, he'd been so sweet. So loving. And I hadn't been afraid at all. Instead, I'd just known, without a shadow of doubt, that he was different from all the others.

"That's... that's..."

He didn't seem to be able to find any words, so I jumped in to fill in the sentence for him. "What? Horrible? Terrible?"

"A miracle," he breathed, and pulled me into his embrace, holding me tight against his body.I closed my eyes, rested my head on his chest and sighed.

Sighed away the stress, the disbelief and the hurt.

I'd made it. I'd found him. The Alpha. My baby's daddy.

And it didn't seem like he planned to send me packing.

"Ah, Tayte." Nevaeh's Alpha, Grayson, cleared his throat. "How about you take your mate home? Get her some new clothes at the shop sometime today, and sort out your pack?"

When I pulled back from Tayte's warm embrace, I could sense storm clouds rolling in.

Not literally. These storm clouds were metaphorical ones. Centered firmly around the other two in Tayte's mini-pack, Sam and Dane.

Uh oh.

Nevaeh had said something about this being a triad of sorts.

"Um..." I wasn't quite sure what to say, but Tayte cut across my bumbling non-answer.

"Good idea, Gray," he said. "Thanks. And Nevaeh, thank you. We owe you. Like, big time."

Nevaeh laughed. "Yeah, yeah, just look after her."

"Goes without saying," Tayte said gruffly, before hustling me out of the house and onto the road. Sam and Dane followed quickly, as if they didn't want to be left behind, but their shoulders were rigid and neither of the other two were smiling.

I shivered with the cold of the early morning air, and everything I'd been through recently.

"So, where to now?" I asked, looking at the three men gathered around me.

"Ah... I think we need to go home and talk about everything," Tayte said, his gaze going to the other two men.

"Okay." That sounded sensible to me. "Where's that?"

I looked around at the clean streets and well-built homes.

The town was incredibly impressive. I hoped I would get the chance to stay here for a while and explore.

"This place is amazing." I sighed. "So fresh and well-maintained."

Though the grass was a little sparse and the town's main street clearly small and lacking in a range of amenities, I assumed that was due to the lack of females born to the pack in this generation.

It still kicked the ass off anything the bears had.

"This way." Tayte put a hand in the small of my back and I had to suppress a shiver of delight at his touch. We began walking along the street. There were more solidly built houses all the way along our route, and a group of shops were clustered in the center around what looked like a town square area.

The shops included clothing stores, a supermarket and a barber.

"I heard whispers about you guys from the bears."

"What did they say?" Tayte asked as the other two walked closely behind us.

Listening, probably, but not wanting to talk yet.

"Well, they said you couldn't have children anymore because there were no females born. Not for a whole generation."

Tayte nodded. "Yes, our mothers were some of the last females born to the pack. Wolf shifters, too. We thought that meant that we'd never have a fated mate, but it seems like the future of the pack lies with humans."

"Like me?" I asked, staring up at his handsome face.

He was so much better looking than I remembered.

My memory had not been kind enough to the strength of his jaw, his funky haircut or his caring eyes.

"Yes, like you." He squeezed my waist a little, then stopped suddenly.

"Grayson said to get you something to wear, but I don't think the shops open until nine-ish."

He looked toward the other two men, who shook their heads.

"Okay, then we'll head home and come back later for that."

"That would be great. Thank you. The last thing I thought about when I ran from the bears was bringing clothes with me."

And what I wore were some of the only decent ones, anyway, so it was no loss.

"You did an incredible thing, Celeste. Escaping them."

I could hear the admiration in Tayte's tone, but I shrugged. I didn't deserve that much praise.

"I didn't really have a choice. I had to protect my baby. And I had to find you."

He smiled at me with all the love I'd hoped for. "I'm glad you did."

We kept walking, and I began to feel strange. My stomach tightened and jumped around in excitement. Not a normal feeling for me.

Amazingly, I could sense no morning sickness or nausea this morning, which was unusual.

Whether it was due to the after-effects of adrenaline from my frantic overnight run, or the sickness had simply run its course and passed, I was unsure. Either way, I was grateful for the small respite.

"Which one is your house?" I asked as I pulled my hands into my sleeves and curled my fingers into fists to keep the warmth inside.

Assuming they had their own house? I wasn't sure how it all worked out here. Nothing about this place felt in any way similar to the life I'd led with the bears.

"Are you cold?" Tayte asked.

"Ah, a little. I'm not used to being outside very much. All my jobs kept me inside."

And I was always moving, scrubbing, cleaning, or running from someone yelling at me. I wasn't used to the fresh air, nor so little fear.

"No problem. We're not far now." He wrapped an arm around my shoulders and the gesture felt natural and comforting. We walked toward a large double-story house, similar to Nevaeh's home from the outside.

But this one seemed wider, and there was more brickwork visible to the eye.

"Is this it? It's beautiful." I stared up at the house that could very soon be my home. "It's like... a house out of a magazine."

I sometimes looked at the magazines in the stand at Walmart when I went shopping for the den.

Tayte opened the front door for me and gestured.

"Welcome."

Wow.

I looked back at Sam and Dane, who were watching me closely but still keeping their distance. I gave them both a small smile, then turned back to the house and took a step closer to the entrance. Tayte suddenly whisked me up into his arms.

I clung to his huge shoulders, pressing into his warmth. "What's happening? What are you doing?"

He chuckled and held me tight. "I'm carrying you across the threshold. Isn't that what you humans do when you mate?"

Heat flushed up my face as he carried me into the lovely home.

It was even bigger inside than it had looked, with twelve-foot high ceilings and huge, male-sized couches.

"Ah... well, I grew up with shifters, and we aren't mated yet..." I swallowed, waiting for the reproach for speaking out of turn, but nothing came.

So, after a few seconds, I continued. "But it's a beautiful gesture. Thank you."

My stomach gurgled loudly. I gasped, putting my hands to my belly.

Tayte grinned. "You're hungry. What can we get you?"

I swallowed hard as acid reflux made my mouth taste terrible.

"I have trouble keeping anything down at the moment. But if you have some water? Or plain crackers."

The smallest of the three men—Dane, I remembered him being introduced as in Nevaeh's house before I fainted—marched over to the kitchen and pulled out a box.

He brought the packet back and handed it to me without saying a word.

"Thank you, Dane."

He was clearly annoyed, and although I wasn't sure exactly why, I knew I was the cause of it. And that upset me. Enough to make my stomach flip.

I took the cracker box. "I'm sorry. I seem to have done something wrong."

His face softened and his shoulders dropped, relaxing a little.

"It's not your fault. I know... I'm just..." He looked at Tayte and the other one. Sam, I remembered.

I felt drawn to touch Dane and I wasn't sure why. Perhaps an unconscious need to ease his obvious pain? But why?

"What is it?" I asked, my hand half-lifting.

Instead of touching Dane, my hand was grabbed by Tayte, who dragged me to the couch.

"Have a seat and we'll explain what's going on."

I sat where he told me, amazed to find the furniture so new. So clean. And it wasn't just the furniture. The whole house was spotless. Not a cigarette butt or a beer bottle in sight.

I crossed my legs and grabbed some crackers from the box, chomping on them and moaning softly when they settled the churning in my belly.

Maybe I'd been too hasty in assuming my morning sickness had disappeared?

"Okay. I'm ready," I said, staring at them all. The three men stood before me like lecturers. Large, medium and smaller-sized. Each incredibly handsome, but in completely different ways.

My stomach suddenly began to churn for a whole different reason. I lowered my gaze to the floor, trying to control the heat that leached up from my neck into my cheeks.

"Ah…" Tayte stopped and Sam rolled his eyes.

No one was talking, so I decided I may as well help them.

They seemed lost.

"Nevaeh told me that in this wolf pack all the men have been put into male triad families."

"Yes." Tayte nodded. "An Alpha." He pointed to himself. "A Beta." He pointed to Sam, and then gestured at Dane. "And an Omega."

I grinned. "The perfect combination."

"The perfect family," Tayte said. "All we need is our fated mate to complete us."

"And that's me?" I asked.

None of this was surprising me. Quite the opposite. It was reinforcing what I'd already heard about the wolf shifters' fated mates, and what Nevaeh had said.

I wasn't scared of these guys. On the contrary, I already trusted them. My gut instinct told me they would never hurt me. And I was more than a little fascinated.

Tayte's eyebrows lifted up and down. "Well... yes. You don't seem phased by any of this."

I bit on another cracker and chewed. "I'm not."

"Ah, not that I'm complaining, but why not?" Tayte asked. "Most humans would freak out at pretty much every aspect of this situation."

I shrugged. "I already knew about the shifter world that exists alongside the human world. I've lived in it practically my whole life. And I knew that you guys were doing the male triad thing. I don't mind looking after you all. My job back at the den was to clean an entire apartment block. Forty-six apartments." I allowed a touch of pride to enter my voice. That was a lot of apartments. "And I can cook, too."

Three men would be easy to look after. I wasn't used to the sex side of things, but I could learn.

Surely, it couldn't be that hard.

Tayte's mouth kicked up at the corners. "You think we want a... housekeeper?"

I looked from Tayte to Sam and then to Dane, surprised by how happy and relaxed I felt in their presence. I wasn't sure I could trust this feeling. I didn't know them. They could be as violent and horrible as the bears if I gave them enough trust. But I kept going with my gut instinct, which told me this situation was nothing like what I had just fled.

To be honest, I didn't have much choice, not with the bears' edict for death, and my pregnancy. So, I was willing to give these three wolves everything I had, in the hopes it would be enough for them to keep me. And my baby.

At least it might be enough for us to be safe.

"Well, yes." Finally, I answered Tayte's query. "Isn't that the role? Housekeeper?"

Tayte began to laugh and so did the other two.

"She's too beautiful to be believed," Sam said, collapsing into a chair.

Well, that was a nice compliment. Maybe he wouldn't turn on me if I kept talking.

I looked at him. "Sam, why are you all laughing at me?"

He smiled broadly. "Because we thought we'd have to convince you to mate with all of us, and you seem ready to jump straight into the role."

He grinned again and my belly tightened. Not with nausea this time, but with an arousal I'd never felt outside that one night with Tayte.

Sam was gorgeous, too, and that smile of his was amazing.

So was Dane's, when I turned to study him, too.

Three sexy guys, all staring at me, waiting for my response to a question I wasn't sure I had gotten right.

"Well..." I didn't quite know how to process the fact that they all wanted me. At least, I think that's what he was saying.

After years of being rejected by every member of the den where I grew up, the idea of three men all wanting to mate with me was as confusing as it was flattering.

"I can't guarantee I can satisfy you all in the..." I swallowed hard. "I've only had, you know, the one time... with Tayte. But anyway." I put my hands to my burning cheeks, covering the evidence of how embarrassing I found this situation.

"I don't expect you guys to be faithful. The bears never were to their mates. But I'll do my best to satisfy you."

The mood in the room changed instantly.

One moment the guys were smiling and laughing, the next they fell silent.

I shivered at the sudden drop in temperature.

"Did I say something wrong?"

"Ah, yeah." Tayte stood up and began to pace. "Fuck, this is a mess." He stopped and sighed.

The disappointment coming off him hit me like a slap to the face.

I tucked my knees up against my chest and wrapped my arms around my legs.

Tears tingled my eyes. "I'm sorry. I didn't mean to upset you."

How had I made such a big mistake already?

Sam moved slowly over to my side.

I put my head on my knees and looked at him sideways.

"Celeste, you didn't upset us. And we didn't mean to upset you. Quite the opposite. So, let me explain a few things to you. As a pack, a family, we've been waiting for you, our fated mate, for years. When Dane and I touched you before, you responded to our touch in a way that means you're our fated mate too, just as much as you are Tayte's."

Tears slipped down my face and I wiped them against my jeans.

"Okay." I didn't know what else to say. I already knew that, so why were they upset? "I mean... that's good, isn't it?"

I still don't understand.

Sam went on. "And although we love the idea of you looking after our home for us—we're terrible at cooking and all those things—that's not why we want you. We know you already want Tayte. You've gone to bed with him... you're pregnant by him, but we…" Sam swallowed, and I could see the pain in his eyes.

Dane walked across the room and sat next to me too, sighing heavily. "Sam and I need you to want us, too. We don't want you to… you know, put up with us just because you have to."

I looked from one beautiful man to the other.

"You both want me?" I lifted my head so I could study them properly.

"Of course, we do."

"For… everything? You don't want to date other women?"

I couldn't believe that was possible. All the bear males cheated on their mates, all the time.

Dane laughed. "Are you kidding me? I never want another filthy one-night-stand ever again. I want a mate; we all do. But how can you really want us, after…"

He trailed off, glancing up at Tayte, whose massive frame towered over us all.

Were they worried I wouldn't care for them after I'd met their Alpha?

I bit my lip, wanting to reassure them, but not totally under-standing what their fears were. "Um… Tayte and I have barely even talked. We met in a bar, when I was blind drunk, depressed and seeking companionship to keep the loneliness at bay."

Dane's gaze dropped and I reached out to hold his hand. Tingles of awareness and attraction pulsed along his palm into mine. "What is that?"

He smiled softly, dimples pressing into his cheeks.

"I think it's something to do with us being fated mates," he said.

"That's awesome. It feels… good."

"It feels very good, beautiful."

I stroked his palm, running my finger along the lines bisecting the flesh.

"So, what do we do now, Dane?"

"What would you like to do, Celeste?"

"Um…" I looked from one man to the other.

I wanted to curl up in a ball and feel their protection all around me. But how could I be honest about that?

"Um…"

"You can tell us."

Could I really? There was only one way to find out.

I took a breath and gathered my courage.

"I want to cuddle. All together. Could we do that?"

Tayte chuckled and the other two grinned. "We can do anything you want, sweetheart, although I'm not sure these two are going to be able to stop themselves from ravishing you."

Oh my God, seriously?

I blushed, heat flooding my cheeks once again.

I still couldn't believe they all wanted me like *that*, instead of just as a housekeeper. After feeling ugly for so long, these three made me feel so sexy and wanted.

I was twenty-three years old and I'd had sex *once*. It was wrong. I wanted to remedy that, but how?

"I… don't mind if you want to. I… you know I've only had sex once. I wouldn't know where to even begin."

The men around me chuckled. "I would," Sam said from next to me. "Come with us, beautiful."

I let him drag me to my feet and tow me up the stairs.

My heart was in my throat, panic pulsing along my veins. The idea of being with three men at once made me want to vomit. Not from disgust, but from fear of disappointing them.

But I had to push the fear down and trust the fated mate link. Even though I had no idea what I was doing when it came to sex.

Sam tugged me into a huge bedroom.

"This is Tayte's room. It has the largest bed."

I glanced around. It was nice, but so male.

So plain, and blue.

I shivered as they drew me to the bed and began to undress themselves.

All three of them were about to be naked and I didn't know where I was supposed to look, or what I should do.

My stomach quivered and I wrapped my arms across my middle.

Tayte gently took one of my hands in his. "It's fine, sweetheart. Let's just lie down and we'll hold you. Don't worry, no one's going to seduce you today."

I looked around the group and expected sullen glares.

Instead, Sam smiled and Dane stared at me with nothing but hope in his expression.

The lack of censure over my obvious nerves made me want to try. For them. And for myself.

"I don't mind." My tone was shy, but hopefully they could hear the truth in my voice. "Like I said, I'll never reject any of you. If you really want me."

Tayte chuckled. "Come to bed, sweetheart, and explain all this to us."

In the end, the men kept their jeans on, climbing into the bed half-clothed instead of fully naked.

Even so, there was still plenty of naked flesh to feast my eyes on. I stared at them, blinded by the huge muscles and clear, tanned skin.

"You guys are so... perfect."

Dane chuckled and Sam grinned.

"What do you mean?" I asked.

"Come here, beautiful." Dane invited me with a gesture of his hand.

He was by far the smallest, and his belly was like slices of granite. Perfectly square and hard, though less intimidating than Sam or Tayte.

I went to him and lay on the bed next to Dane.

They moved around me and it felt like a warm cloud enveloping me.

I lay on top of Dane and the other two kept their hands on me.

My heart raced and I tried to settle it down by breathing deeply.

I waited for them to make their moves. To have sex with me.

But they didn't.

They just stroked me, held me, and sighed beneath me.

I couldn't believe it. Finally, I let myself relax, the tension in my muscles releasing into the room and somehow floating away.

"Tell us where this fear of acceptance and everything is coming from, Celeste. Tell us your story," Tayte said, kissing my shoulder and tucking a stray lock of hair away from my face.

So, I did.

I told them about me growing up thinking I belonged in the

bear den, only to discover I was a human they'd found in the woods, years ago.

That none of them had wanted me, even the lowest of all the bear shifters. Of the disgust that the bears had shown toward me. Of all my years of servitude and struggle, and the anger and rage and moments of physical aggression that had led to broken bones and bruising.

I talked about how I'd finally had the chance to get out, and had gone to the bar that night to drown my sorrows.

That night, I'd found Tayte.

"And Tayte actually wanted me." I still couldn't believe it, and some of that disbelief must have been evident in my voice.

He laughed where he lay beside me, his leg thrown over mine. "Of course, I did. You were, and still are, beautiful, sweet, and quite obviously as lonely as I was."

I lifted my head off Dane's chest so I could look down at him.

"How come you guys thought I wouldn't want you?"

Dane ran his hand along my arm.

"Well, you've already been with our Alpha. I was worried we wouldn't be able to compete."

I smiled, hope filling me up like a waterfall into a tiny spring.

"And I assumed no man would ever want me. And that you three would have to *endure* me for the sake of the baby."

"Endure?" Sam's voice was a murmur.

Dane's hand slid down to cup my belly. My breath caught in my throat at the tender caress. It was the first time another person had recognized my pregnancy in a positive way.

He didn't say anything at that point, but I knew he wanted to talk about the coming baby. How did he and Sam feel about me having the Alpha's baby?

"Is it... I mean... Are you and Sam upset that I'm going to have a baby?" I turned my head to look at Tayte. "Are you upset about it, too?"

Tayte's exclamation echoed through the room. "Our baby is a miracle come true, Celeste!"

His sincerity shone in his eyes.

As much as I loved seeing that, his enthusiasm didn't mean the others felt the same way.

Tayte rubbed my thigh. "You know how we feel."

I glanced at Sam, who was being very quiet, then to Dane. "I know Tayte's okay with it, but what about you two? How does it work? Shall I have a baby with each of you, too?"

I didn't mind the idea. I wouldn't want anyone to feel left out.

Dane swallowed "We'd love that... but..."

He glanced at Sam, who finally said, "We want this baby to be ours, too. Not just Tayte's."

"Oh." That sounded amazing. "So, you want to adopt it, or something?"

Tayte chuckled. "We're a pack, sweetheart. Like Grayson and Dexter's pack. Claire's pregnant and they don't know whose babies she's carrying. They're simply the packs' babies. And they will all love them, equally."

Sam nodded. "We would have liked to be there too, the night this gorgeous baby was conceived, and next time you get pregnant, we're going to have to insist, I'm afraid." He grinned at me and I couldn't help but smile back. What a beautiful concept.

He continued. "But if you accept us as your mates, then we're going to say this baby is ours."

I looked at Dane. "Do you feel that way, too?"

He grinned, those sexy dimples coming out to play. "Of

course. I'm not missing out on being called Daddy for another five years while I wait for my turn."

I looked from one man to the next.

"Are you serious? You all want to be my mate? And you all want to be my baby's daddy? Like... seriously?"

I'd definitely died, because this couldn't be real. Three hot, sexy and caring men who wanted to mate with me, and claim my baby as theirs?

After so many years of being alone, watching other people get married and have babies, and being shunned by a whole pack, I couldn't comprehend that this might be my new reality.

I could be happy here. Like, *really* happy.

No way could I have found my own version of heaven. Could I?

The chuckles around me rose and fell.

"Why are you all laughing?"

Tayte turned my face toward his with a tug of my chin. "Because, sweetheart, we're the ones who feel lucky to have found you. And it sounds like you feel the same way."

"Of course, I do!" I practically yelled at them. "The bears hated me. I knew it, even as a child. But I was a good worker, and strong for my size. It was the only reason they kept me."

"As a slave," Tayte said, his voice becoming dark and flat.

"Well... yes."

I almost added, *because what else is there*? But then I held back the words. Because, with these men, the possibility of knowing something bigger and better was right at the edge of my experience. I may not have ever known anything different, but perhaps it was possible to dream of something better in the future.

"Those days are gone, sweetheart," Tayte said. "In this home you will have equal say, equal rights, and more love, sex and attention than you'll know what to do with."

I glanced from one gorgeous face to another.

It sounded too good to be true. And yet...

"Sounds perfect."

Tayte turned my face toward him and drew me close for a kiss.

CHAPTER

FIVE

DANE

Tayte was already kissing her. Our mate. Sam stared at me like he was asking, "What the hell do we do?"

I shrugged. I had no idea.

I'd never had an orgy before, if this situation could even be labeled like that?

Should we take her separately? Together? I wasn't sure of the rules, and most of all, I didn't want to upset or hurt Celeste.

Sam looked away, a frown marring his face. Clearly, he wasn't coping with this either.

Then our mate, the beautiful girl, reached for me. Her little hand came back and found my arm, squeezing me.

I met Sam's gaze again, saw his eyes on Celeste's grip on me, and grinned at him.

Suddenly, I knew everything was going to be all right.

I lay down behind Celeste and began to kiss her neck. Her scent rose up, so intoxicating that my whole body switched itself on.

55

She moaned and gasped, arching her neck as if she enjoyed my lips there, and this time reached over Tayte for Sam.

The energy in the room flipped like a switch.

It went from simmering to scalding in an instant.

Tayte slid off the bed and stood up. I glanced at him.

He said, "I think we should mate with her. All together. But as I've already been with Celeste, you two need to bond more strongly. I'll wait and watch for a bit."

I couldn't believe the Alpha was offering her to us, but I wasn't going to wait for him to change his mind.

I set my lips back on her neck and ran my hands around to her front, cupping her breasts and aching to strip her.

"That's so good, Dane," she moaned, then reached again for Sam who was now lying in front of her. "Sam, I want you, too."

I looked up and met his gaze over the top of her. He seemed torn, his brow furrowed down and his mouth a straight line.

"I..." He started to speak and then stopped. I knew what was in his mind, because part of me was worried about the same thing.

Celeste moaned again, softly. "You don't want to?"

Sam shook his head. "Of course, I do. But if *you* don't.... I can't..."

I whispered into Celeste's ear. "He's worried you're doing this out of obligation."

Celeste released a shocked little breath, then sat up and crawled closer to Sam. She touched his arm, traced her fingers over his chest, and I saw him shiver.

"You know I'm the virgin, right? Well, sort of," she whispered.

He nodded.

"Then you're going to have to teach me. I'm sorry, I have no idea how to show you that I want you, too. Or you, Dane." She glanced over her shoulder and smiled shyly my way, before turning back to Same. "Other than to say, please don't leave me. I couldn't handle the rejection. Not after everything."

Sam groaned loudly, and then crushed her to him, kissing her upturned lips and gripping her body tight, as if he never wanted to let her go.

I slid off the bed and walked around to the side where Sam held her.

I stripped off my jeans and knelt to pull her joggers off. But I couldn't get to her legs properly, not with the way she was draped all over Sam.

I tapped his leg. "Sam. Help me."

He pulled back and, when he saw what I was doing, helped Celeste to stand. Together, we removed her clothes until she was naked and shivering.

Wow.

She was damn beautiful. Thin, with the pregnancy not yet showing, but so feminine and soft.

"Am I... all right?" she asked, as she glanced down at her body.

I moaned as I stood up behind her and pressed my aching cock into the small of her back.

"You..." I grunted, cupping her perfect little breasts with my hands, "are fucking perfect." I thrust against her so she could feel how hard I was for her.

She leaned into me as Sam stripped.

I heard her gasp at seeing him and grinned as I kissed her back and shoulders.

I didn't know how we were going to take this slow enough for her, but we had to try.

"Lie down, beautiful. On the bed," I said.

She slid onto the sheets and lay there still for a moment, before covering her small breasts with her hands.

I looked at Sam, the Beta of my pack, waiting for his lead.

I didn't know what he liked to do, or not, in bed. We'd never actually discussed it. But I had a feeling the topic was going to become normal breakfast conversation from now on.

"You want top or bottom?"

"Bottom."

Hmm... I was surprised. I liked the bottom, too. For some reason I'd assumed he'd be the opposite to me.

I nodded and, being the Omega of the group, allowed him first choice as I crawled over to Celeste on the bed.

"Hello, beautiful. We're going to make love to you now, is that all right?"

She nodded, shivering where she lay, waiting for us. I ran my fingers over her curves, wanting to make sure her shivers were from arousal and not fear. She moaned and arched into my touch, her cheeks flushing with a delicate pink and goose bumps rising up on her flesh in the wake of my fingers.

"Oh, that feels so good, Dane. To be touched, with loving hands..."

Definitely arousal.

"You say stop, at any point, and we stop, okay?" I wanted her to understand that she had the power and control in this situation. "Time out."

She nodded again and I couldn't stop myself from kissing her, everywhere.

Kissing her upturned lips, her nose, her cheeks.

Every part of her exquisite face.

Bending further and taking one, then the other, of her beautiful nipples into my mouth and suckling. Then I released her beautiful breasts and raised my face to her again.

"Okay?" I repeated, so she knew. "We're serious. You ask us to stop, and we stop. No matter what. We're going to be together for a very long time, so we can wait. Forever, if that's what it takes."

Tears welled in her brilliant blue eyes, then slid down her cheeks.

"Can you kiss me again, please? *Ah...*"

Her eyes widened and her mouth fell open in a gasp.

I looked down her body.

Sam was lying on his belly between her thighs and looking up at her.

His finger was circling her clit. I groaned as more heat flooded my groin at seeing her perfect little pussy open like that for the first time, her legs wide and her mound lifting up as if to press harder into Sam's finger.

I swooped down to kiss her lips as Sam leaned in and began to eat her.

She gasped and groaned against my lips, arching her back in pleasure.

I took the opportunity and slid my tongue into her mouth.

Tasting her tongue in return. Loving her groans as they vibrated in my mouth and throat.

She grabbed for my back, digging her nails into my skin until I groaned myself.

I moved down her divine little body. Suckling her nipples

again, until they turned into tight little pebbles and she threaded her fingers into my hair as if to hold me in place.

She was crying out, her belly shuddering with Sam's ministrations on her pussy.

I glanced down and jealousy swept through me.

I moved down and nudged him. "My turn."

He came up for air and licked his lips, wetness glistening on his face.

"Sure."

He crawled up beside her and dove down on her mouth, kissing her and squeezing her breasts.

I opened her legs wider to see all of her perfect pussy. She was wet, the petals of her sex open and swollen in arousal.

I ducked my head and set my lips around her clit, licking and suckling at her flesh until she was screaming out to me.

I slid a finger inside her pussy, her tight muscles gripping and squeezing me.

Fuck... I couldn't wait to feel those same muscles tighten around my cock.

I worked her from the inside, then added a second finger, stretching her for us. I thrust in and out of her wet channel until she was writhing beneath my hand, screaming for me.

"Fuck it."

I couldn't wait any longer. Her body needed me.

She needed me.

And I'd never needed a woman more.

I crawled up between her thighs and lay down on top of her.

Sam moved out of the way as I lifted her legs and positioned my cock at her entrance.

My balls ached and my belly tightened with need. I had to have her.

I grabbed the shaft and ran the head up and down over her swollen clit and around her entrance.

She lifted her legs higher, tilting her pelvis up to me in wordless invitation.

"Are you ready to take me, beautiful?"

She nodded.

I waited. "I need you to say it."

I never wanted my mate to regret this moment. And I needed her to see that I was in full control of my lust, and could stop at any time. If she wanted me to.

It would kill me to do so, but I'd do anything to make her happy.

"Yes, please."

Those were the sweetest words I'd ever heard in my life.

I growled as I reset my cock at her entrance and gently thrust inside.

She gasped and moaned, her eyes going wide.

Then she arched up to me, making it almost impossible to move slowly.

"Oh, fuck." I gripped the sheets beneath her and forged inside. Into the tightest, sweetest, most perfect pussy I'd ever felt.

"Dane. Oh, Dane."

She was kissing my throat, my shoulders. Desperately. Lovingly.

I couldn't take much more of it. I was about to explode.

I allowed some of my weight to drop down onto her, loving the heat of her skin against mine. Her soft breasts pressed against my chest.

I began to move, thrusting in and out of her delicious body. The heat of her was indescribable, and the tightness... wow. It was like a hand-made glove, a perfect fit, squeezing me.

I wanted the sensation to go on forever, but I was never going to last.

She was too perfect, and I'd waited too long for her already.

I ducked my head, tasting her lips and using all my control to take her slowly, carefully.

But she was gripping me so tightly, so beautifully.

"I'm sorry, beautiful, but I'm never going to last. You're making me... come."

The heat flared up my back and through my belly.

I thrust a little harder and squeezed my muscles tight, trying to hold on.

But then she tilted her pelvis, taking me even deeper, and I was gone.

The hottest, most intense orgasm of my life was about to explode through my body and I had to let it out.

I began to ride her harder, thrusting into her and hearing her squeaks and moans of pleasure.

She wrapped her legs around my waist and whispered, "Please come for me."

I couldn't hold back after that. I thrust once more, deep into her belly.

The roar ripped through me as my seed pulsed into her in hot, long streams.

She gasped and dug her nails into my back, squeezing my cock with her channel walls and making the orgasm extend on and on.

I kissed her face, her neck, then relaxed onto her, trying to keep most of my weight up and off her.

But, fucking hell, it was amazing.

I hadn't realized I'd closed my eyes, but as I opened them and looked down on her, she smiled up at me. Beamed, actually.

"Are you okay?" I asked, my voice hoarse.

She nodded. "Oh, yeah. That was great."

Sam tapped me on the back. *Damn*. My time was at an end.

I kissed her lips once more.

A pathetic effort on my behalf, but luckily, I had back-up. "There's a lot more to come, beautiful."

I slid off her sweet body and rolled to the side.

Sam grabbed her legs and hauled her to the edge of the bed.

She squealed and laughed as he lifted her up and put pillows under her ass.

"Ready for me?" Sam asked her, his voice gravelly and dark. He was not going to last long either, it seemed. Not this first time, at least.

She smiled up at him, wiggling on the pillows as if eager for more.

She hadn't found release yet, but hopefully she would, soon.

Sam grabbed his cock, lined himself up, and thrust straight into her.

Celeste moaned and arched up.

Sam didn't go slowly.

He rode her fast, and hard, and deep.

The thwacking sounds as their flesh met made my gut tighten with renewed heat.

I knelt on the bed and caressed her hard nipples as she moaned and cried out.

Her face contorted and she began to gasp, as if she was right on the precipice of an orgasm.

Sam gave a strangled groan and then thrust forward once more, coming inside our mate just as fiercely as I had, judging by the shudders and moans coming from him.

Celeste was shuddering, too, clawing at the bed.

Sam pulled away, gasping for air.

And then Tayte stepped up.

Celeste blinked up at him, her skin flushed and her eyes brilliant with unsated desire. "Tayte... I need..."

"I know, sweetheart. Get on your knees. We're all here."

She rolled off the pillows, her soft skin shining with a thin film of sweat. Herlegs shook as she stood, then turned and knelt back on the bed for him.

Presenting her ass to the Alpha.

"I think she needs all three of us to make her come. Don't you sweetheart?"

Celeste bent down, pressing her face into the bedcovers, and said, "I don't know. I don't know..."

She was practically sobbing.

"Dane, Sam, touch her, push her to the highest limits."

Sam and I knelt either side of her and began to kiss her wherever we could reach.

Her neck, her back. Her beautiful shoulders. I pushed her hair to the side and nuzzled at her neck. Then I reached beneath her and cupped one of her breasts, the soft flesh filling my palm.

Sam cupped her other one, massaging it, then reached behind her and thrust the fingers of his other hand into her.

She cried out and gasped.

Tayte stood behind us, his eyes glittering with arousal. He was stroking himself, getting ready for her.

"My turn." His voice was a command.

Sam instantly withdrew his fingers and lay down beside our mate. I lay down on her other side, biting on her shoulder and licking her ear.

I heard the grunt and felt the thrust as Tayte filled her up.

"More. Please," Celeste begged.

He wasn't moving, I realized. Not at first.

But at Celeste's request, and another repeated beg, finally he began to fuck her.

Their bodies banged together until she screamed out to him. To Sam. And to me.

I reached beneath her and worked her swollen clit with my fingers, in circles.

Over and over.

Sam kissed her face and neck. Then she began to arch and gasp, her whole body bowing up as she began one long crescendo of sound.

And then it released like an arrow. Hard and fast and hitting center.

She shook and shuddered and cried out, grabbing hold of me and Sam, impaled by Tayte, and anchoring herself with all three of us surrounding her.

I looked over at Sam, who was holding her hand, too, then up at Tayte. That's when I felt the energy connection flowing between all four of us.

It was a moment that almost stopped my heart.

That made me feel whole.

Then it was Tayte's turn to tip over the edge.

Celeste cried out again, softer this time as Tayte roared and came inside her.

The three us had spilled our seed inside her, our genetics mixing together in her womb.

The way it should have been from the start.

The thought made me wonder if things would ever be equal between us. Would Celeste ever love me and Sam, or need us, as much as she did Tayte? The acknowledged father of her child.

The Alpha collapsed beside her, panting and gasping for breath.

I reached for her as she fell forward on the mattress, her eyes closed and her body obviously exhausted. She drifted into sleep as I watched.

I didn't really want to stay in Tayte's bed any longer.

I needed some space.

I loved being an Omega, a part of this family, but I wasn't sure how I was going to ever compete for an equal share of my mate's love with the Alpha around.

"I'm going to have a shower."

Sam stood up. "Me too." Possibly, he felt the same way.

Tayte scooped our mate up and held her against him. "I don't think she should be alone while she sleeps."

"Yeah, true. See you later, then."

Sam and I left, and Celeste slept on.

She didn't stir, obviously not noticing even on an unconscious level that we were gone, and I didn't blame her. Not really.

"So much for this being an equal relationship, huh?" Sam said as we headed to our end of the house.

"I'm gonna have a shower. You okay if I go first?"

I cringed a little as I asked the question. I was requesting permission to shower first, and yet I hadn't asked whether he cared if I made love to our mate first.

Seemed stupid somehow.

Sam shrugged and didn't look at me. "Whatever. Doesn't matter to me."

He went into his bedroom and shut the door.

A cold fist tightened inside my gut.

Damn it. How did this day turn from good to bad so quickly?

I went into the bathroom and had a long, hot shower, washing away the smell of my mate and of the sex we'd enjoyed together.

Hoping in a strange way that if I did that, I could wash away the feelings of imbalance and inadequacy as well.

After I was dry and dressed, I realized it was going to take a lot more than a shower to get rid of that feeling of rejection.

I woke up to cramping and pain.

"Oh, no." I grabbed for my stomach. "The baby."

Tayte, who'd been asleep beside me, jumped up out of bed and stared down at me with a shocked look on his face. "What's wrong?"

Panic gripped my heart as my belly tightened once again. "I think it's the baby."

I couldn't be miscarrying! No! Not after everything I had risked to keep it safe.

"Fuck! What do we do?"

Tayte was already pulling on jeans.

I didn't know. What should we do?

"Um... do you have a doctor here?"

I checked between my legs. There was a lot of wetness.

But I wasn't bleeding. Not yet.

"Claire! Let's get you to Claire." Tayte grabbed for my clothes and helped me dress, then scooped me up into his arms and ran down the stairs.

I clung to him, but my grief sat on top of me like a cloud.

He called to the others, "Sam! Dane! We gotta go."

Dane came running at the sound of Tayte's voice. "What's wrong?"

I sobbed when I saw him and reached out for my sweet Omega. "Dane..."

Worry shadowed his expression and he grabbed my hands.

"She's cramping," Tayte said. "There's something wrong with the baby."

Sam walked into the room as Tayte spoke and I saw his face pale when he heard the words.

The cramps hit again, the tightness and pain making me cry out. "Ow!" And another sob left my throat. "Oh, no. I'm going to lose it, aren't I?"

Tayte dropped a kiss on top of my head.

Sam ran to the front door and wrenched it open. "Let's go."

They ran with me through the town and I clung to Tayte, burying my face in the crook of his neck and breathing in the comforting scent of him.

What had I done wrong?

Was it because I'd run away last night?

Or because I'd let all three of them make love to me at once?

Or was this always going to happen because I was a weak little female who couldn't handle a strong baby like Tayte's?

They rushed me inside a house I hadn't seen before.

"Claire! Help!" Tayte's voice was urgent, and a nice-looking woman came rushing forward to greet us. This must be the doctor, Claire, that I'd heard so much about. She looked a little older than me.

She frowned when she saw me in Tayte's arms and quickly showed us into a small bedroom off the lounge area.

"Put her down on the bed, please, Tayte. Now, what's happened?" she asked.

All three men started talking at once and Claire stopped them with a wave of her hand. "You three go out and cool off. I'll help your mate, okay?"

She literally shoved them out the door and I called out, suddenly too worried to be left alone with a stranger.

Human or not.

"No! Please. Can Dane stay?"

I didn't know why I called only for Dane, but his calm strength was what I wanted in this moment.

He'd been the first to make love to me today.

The first one to kiss me.

The first one to look into my eyes and make me feel incredibly loved.

Dane looked at his pack mates, unspoken words passing between them. Then he nodded and rushed back to sit by my side and hold my hand.

I clung to him and turned so I could put my head on his lap.

He stroked my hair and I finally felt safe again.

Claire pulled up a chair and sat next to us, studying me.

"Ah... this isn't the exact introduction I was expecting for the newest mate of the pack, but I'm Claire. I'm a doctor at the hospital where Nevaeh works, and I'm pretty sure you're the one who went looking for me last night."

I stared at her from my place in Dane's lap. "Yes, I did. I'm Celeste."

"Hello, Celeste. How can I help you today?"

She was so calm. Her manner was lovely and soothing. I knew she would help me if she could, but if this pregnancy wasn't meant to be, then physician or not, she couldn't save it.

"I... I think I'm losing my baby."

My throat tightened and I swallowed the cry that threatened to rise up.

"How far along are you?"

"Um... about eight weeks." I hadn't seen a doctor of course, but my period was a month late.

"Okay. Are you bleeding?"

"No, not yet. I don't think so."

Claire stood up. "So, why do you think you're losing the baby?"

I gathered my strength and sat up, wiping away the tears that fell down my cheeks.

"I'm..." Another wave of pain hit. "Cramping."

I put a hand on my belly.

"Like you're getting your period?"

I shook my head. "No, worse. It's like a deep soreness."

Dane reached for my hand again and held it tight.

Claire looked between us. "Have you been having sex this morning?"

Dane leaned forward. "Yes. Why? Could that have done something? Is it our fault?"

Claire smiled gently. "No. But from what Nevaeh said, Celeste is very inexperienced, yes?"

She looked at me and despite all the fear in my heart, I found myself smiling. She seemed so kind and trustworthy.

"Ah... yes. Tayte was my first and that was two months ago."

Claire grinned. "And let me guess, all three of them doted on you and made you orgasm this morning, probably for the first time."

Now this conversation was getting embarrassing. I had to remember, she was a doctor. It was all right to discuss these things with your doctor, surely?

"Um, yes."

Dane blinked at me. "You didn't come the first time with Tayte?"

I shook my head. "No, of course not."

Dane looked up at Claire, his mouth open a little.

Claire looked as if she was biting back a smile when she said, "Almost impossible for a virgin. You three did well today, it seems, Dane."

He looked away. "It wasn't me. Or Sam. It was Tayte."

Claire reached over and touched his hand and I turned toward him, too. Was Dane feeling bad about the incredible morning we'd had? How was that possible?

Claire said, "Dane, you don't know much about the mating triad yet, but you'll soon learn that we human, fated mates need all three of our men. All of you, equally. We don't do well without all of you."

I slid my head back into Dane's lap and turned my cheek so I could kiss his leg. "This morning was perfect. You were perfect. You all were. Equally."

There was silence in the air until Dane finally slid his fingers through my hair once again. He seemed more relaxed, suddenly.

"So, Doc, what do we do?" he said. "Does this mean the baby is going to be okay? It's just Celeste's body getting used to the aftermath of an orgasm?"

Claire shrugged. "Look, I'll be honest with you. If Celeste is going to miscarry, there's nothing I can do. Miscarriage is very common, especially in first pregnancies, and it doesn't mean anything is wrong with the woman. It's just... sometimes how things go, sadly. But most women go on to have very normal, healthy second pregnancies."

I pressed my head against my Omega, my heart aching and tears filling my eyes once again. "Maybe it's for the best. I know you and Sam don't like the idea that I'm having just Tayte's baby. I..."

I lost my words again and stopped talking, my throat squeezing shut with tears and pain.

"Oh no, sweetheart, don't say that." Dane pulled me up into his arms and held me as I cried.

It hurt so much.

I'd wanted a family, a baby, for so long, and now it was possible I was going to lose it.

Claire left us alone then, and I kept crying.

Sam came into the room and sat down on the bed with us, stroking my back and putting an arm around me.

Tayte hadn't returned, and I didn't mind too much, at least for a little while.

Sam and Dane provided more than enough love and support.

When my tears dried up, Claire returned to the room and got my attention again.

"I think you three have a bit to talk about, but from a medical perspective, Celeste, I'll tell you this. Rest today. See how things go. If nature decides to take its course, I can advise you then. But if this is what I think it is, which is lots of sex and orgasms in someone not used to it, then you'll be better by tomorrow and have no bleeding. So, watch for blood, and if you're still concerned, I can take you into the hospital tomorrow and do an ultrasound."

I clung to Dane and nodded. "Okay, thank you, Doctor."

Claire waved her hand at me.

"Stay here for a few hours. I have to do a little shopping, and my boys are all out at work, so you'll have the house to yourself."

"Um, is Tayte all right?" I had to ask, given he hadn't yet returned.

"He's fine. I advised him to go make himself useful somewhere else so the three of you can bond for a little while. The triad thing can be hard when there's so many people wanting love and acceptance, but I can already tell that you four will be just fine."

She left and closed the door and I sagged into my men.

"I should probably check if I'm bleeding."

I moved to stand up and Dane grabbed my hand. "Um, before you do, I have to say something."

"Okay."

He looked at Sam and they both seemed so sad.

"What's wrong?"

Sam coughed and cleared his throat.

"We're both... um, struggling with this. That you and Tayte seem so much closer than we could ever hope to be."

A wave of sadness washed over me, dragging me into the darkness.

"So, you're glad I'm going to lose this baby." I nodded my

head, the cramps in my belly continuing, though strangely, they were no longer as sharp.

They were more like the pains of muscle strain now. "Yeah... I suppose..." I wiped at new tears. "We can make more babies."

Dane grunted as if in shock. "Is that what you think?"

Before I could say anything in response, Sam grabbed my hand and pulled me over to him.

"Sit, sweetheart."

I sat on his lap and looped my arms around his neck, putting my head on his chest so I could be as close as possible.

The world was so cold and dark now, when only a few hours ago it had been filled with possibilities and hope.

"Celeste, we do *not* want you to lose your baby."

I pulled away so I could look up at him, his brown eyes intense.

I wiped at the tears that would not stop falling.

"You don't?"

"Of course not. We were excited about being a family so soon."

That part I understood.

"But you... you don't like that you weren't there. And if this baby... goes away, then we can make one together."

I was trying, I was really trying to see the silver lining of this day.

They shared a look that I couldn't read, and horror struck my heart.

"Unless... if you're only keeping me around because I was pregnant, does that mean you'll send me away now, if I lose the baby?"

My arms dropped away from Sam's neck and I began to fall. Fall into the abyss that swirled around me.

I didn't know how I was going to pull myself out of this one.

Where would I even go if these men rejected me?

Sam grabbed for my shoulders and held me to him again, while Dane slid closer and cupped my face.

"Celeste, stop and look at us, okay? We know you've been hurt and betrayed in the past, and been unloved for far too long. But that isn't the case now. Not with us. That will never happen again."

I didn't believe them, but I nodded anyway.

"Okay."

"Listen, and listen closely. We *love* you... do you understand that? We love you. We don't want you to ever leave us. And whether we have one baby, or fifteen, we will love them all. Because they will be a part of you, and us. Our pack."

A sob built in my throat and escaped this time.

"But how..."

"It's the fated mate bond. You are our heaven, our perfection, and we will love you with every breath, every minute of every day. No matter what."

I looked from to Dane to Sam and saw the same stoic strength. The same heart that beat in them both.

"But... you left me this morning; I felt it. You didn't want to stay in the bed with me and Tayte, and I know this baby is unwanted."

Sam growled a little, his chest vibrating with his breath. "Your baby is not unwanted. He or she brought you to us. Without the pregnancy, we may never have found you."

That was probably true, but I still didn't quite believe them.

They were just trying to make me feel better, which said a lot about the strength of their characters and the beauty of their hearts.

"Thank you for saying that."

Sam growled again.

"We aren't just *saying* it—"

Dane burst in with, "We felt rejected, like we were third wheels in the situation. Unwanted add-ons to your relationship with Tayte."

Silence descended as their words sunk in.

Then I began to laugh.

I sounded hysterical, and I probably was.

"Um... you felt... you guys...." I couldn't stop laughing. *They* had felt rejected? By *me?*

I had to get up.

I staggered to my feet, then fell into the chair Claire had placed by the bed.

Dane and Sam stared at me like I'd gone nuts.

"Oh, come on... You two..." I took some deep breaths, forcing myself to breathe, to calm the racing of my heart.

This was a little too hilarious.

"What's funny, Celeste?" Sam asked, his tone bordering on annoyed.

I forced myself to sober quickly. They were beginning to look offended again.

I reached over and held each of their hands.

"You two are super-hot, powerful shifters. I'm just a little, ugly human. Do you know how blessed I feel to have you both? To know that you want me, even a fraction of how much I want you?"

It still seemed totally impossible to me that these men desired me.

Professed to love me.

And would protect me against all enemies.

Sam grinned and Dane's smile was so beautiful, I took a mental picture to capture for all time.

"So... I'm going to the bathroom to see if these cramps mean what I think they mean, and then can you please take me home?"

The men nodded, their concerned faces making my heart sing.

This baby may have been the only reason I escaped the bears, so maybe it was fated on more than one level?

SEVEN

CELESTE

In the end, the cramps subsided and an ultrasound proved the baby was healthy and strong.

Just one little baby was inside me.

Claire was adamant that it was all the sex and the massive orgasm that had caused the cramping.

So, the men didn't touch me.

For weeks.

Until I practically pounced on them and they *had* to make love to me.

But, boy, were they gentle!

Too gentle.

The weeks wore on and I grew bigger and bigger.

My one baby made my appetite skyrocket, and my belly protruded through all the new clothes the boys had bought for me.

But despite the early fear of miscarriage, and the fact that they were all too nervous to touch me in a sexual way, we fell into a beautiful rhythm of sleeping together all night, then I'd wake to one of them bringing me breakfast before they headed off to work.

I'd clean the house, if I felt up to it, and bake for them.

They'd come home at lunchtime to check on me, and Claire and Nevaeh were frequent visitors.

I'd never had female friends before, and it was a lovely addition to my life.

Especially all the mothers-in-law.

Three of them.

All pleased as punch to have a grandchild on the way.

And the best part of all?

We hadn't heard a thing from the bears.

They hadn't found me. I was finally beginning to feel safe.

Or at least, I wanted to think I now felt safe, but when the door opened one lunchtime and my heart leapt with stress, as it always did, I realized I had a way to go in that regard. Too many years of watching and waiting for a flying fist still had me jumpy.

As Tayte walked into the house, full of smiles and laughter, I let the anxiety go down a notch.

It was taking longer than I thought it would, to feel safe and "normal".

According to Claire, my version of normal—a Cinderella-type slaving away under a whole bunch of abusive bears—was *not* normal.

A part of me just *knew* that this beautiful dream I was currently living in would shatter sooner or later.

That these lovely, kind wolves would come to their senses and realize I wasn't worth loving, or keeping.

But for now...

"How's my beautiful sweetheart?" Tayte asked as he picked me up and gently twirled me around.

When he put me down, his hand cupped my belly and stroked our baby with a possessive air.

"Have you eaten lunch?"

I shook my head. "No, I've been waiting for you. There's tuna pasta in the oven if you're hungry, or I can just make some sandwiches?"

"If you've cooked a hot lunch already, that would be great."

Sam and Dane came through the front door as I was serving Tayte the pasta.

I got kisses and cuddles from both of them, and the love surrounded me.

I so wanted to accept that this new reality was one that would last.

My men sat at the table and ate, talking about their work and the food I'd made for them.

"This is so good, sweetheart," Tayte said as he finished his second bowl. "Thank you."

I sat and picked at my food.

"You okay, beautiful?" Sam asked.

"Yes. It's funny, I just... you know, no one ever said thank you to me for cooking for them, before. And you guys thank me all the time. I can't quite get my head around it."

Dane jumped up from the table and moved behind me to put his arms around my waist, or what was left of it.

"Oh, beautiful, you deserve compliments for everything you do. The house looks amazing, the food's brilliant, but it's you we come home for. You know the pizza place delivers, right?"

I laughed as he rubbed my belly in soothing circles and my pussy pulsed in response.

I swallowed down the moan.

I'd been holding on to my desires for months.

And I wasn't sure I could keep being the quiet little girl they'd been wrapping in cotton wool, for too much longer.

"Are you going back to work, or...."

Tayte was a builder and both Dane and Sam were bricklayers. That explained the solid house and the incredible facade of our home.

Tayte stood up and cleared the table, then arranged everything in the new dishwasher they'd installed for me. Such luxuries.

I was too spoilt already.

Tayte replied with, "We could go either way. Back to work, or not. Do you need us to do something for you?"

I licked my lips.

I most certainly did.

But could I convince them to stop treating me like I was made of glass?

Since the miscarriage scare, they'd all been too nice to me.

I needed to be *taken*.

I wanted to feel the desire that had built on that first day with the three of them.

The passion, and lust, and need.

Claire, who was even more pregnant than I was, reassured me that it was completely safe for them to—how had she phrased it?—*bang me into next week.*

Heat crept up my neck and into my cheeks. I wasn't sure I could use that phrase here in front of the boys.

Sam grinned at me. "What'cha thinking, gorgeous? You look like you're blushing."

I took a breath and forced myself to get it over and done with.

Surely, they wouldn't reject me?

"I'd like to go to bed, please."

"Bed, as in you're tired? Would you like me to carry you up?" Sam asked, standing quickly.

I almost laughed. Almost. But then frustration took over.

Did I have to strip naked and do a dance to get them to notice my other needs?

How were they so blind?

"No... um, I want you all to make love to me."

Tayte growled with the sexy Alpha noise that was uniquely his, and scooped me up into his arms.

"Well, that we can do."

I clung to his neck as he trotted up the stairs, carrying my weight easily.

I giggled, unable to conceptualize just how crazy this was.

That I was going to have to tell them what I craved.

Tayte set me on my feet in our bedroom and the three men began to undress.

The heat in the room became charged, sizzling with energy.

I pushed my leggings down and pulled my top off. Though they loved to undress me, I wanted to show them how desperate I was.

"Whoa... hang on," Tayte said as I reached for my bra.

But I ignored him and tossed my bra to the ground and pushed my knickers down my legs.

I'd put on weight everywhere in the past three months. My boobs were huge, and my ass had never been so big.

But as the masculine groans sounded around me, I was once again assured that my size didn't seem to turn them off.

Quite the opposite.

Tayte rubbed my back. "Lie down, sweetheart."

I didn't move, though the submissive side of me was anxious to do what the Alpha commanded. I'd been working on denying Tayte. Every day, just one little thing at a time.

It was one of Nevaeh's tips.

For un-programming the things the bears had made me believe and feel about myself, and the world around me.

Asserting myself, and saying no sometimes, was a huge step in that process.

"I'd rather start another way, please."

I dropped to my knees and crawled over to where Tayte stood, already partly aroused in preparation for our session.

"What are you...?"

I wrapped my hand around Tayte's cock and looked up at him.

I wanted to suck him, so much. To feel his hot flesh in my mouth and give him pleasure as much as me. But how did one do that? This was where my inexperience was definitely not my best friend.

Tayte pulled out of my grasp and my fantasy slipped away.

He grabbed my elbows and hauled me to my feet.

"Sweetheart, you don't have to do that."

His face was too kind, too soft. Too understanding.

I didn't want that.

I pulled away.

"Stop it. All of you. I'm not breakable! This baby..." I cupped my belly, "is strong and healthy, and I want you to stop treating me like a *fucking China doll!*"

I'd never spoken to anyone in such a way, let alone three large and muscled men who could beat me to a pulp if they chose to.

My heart pounded and my stomach was tight with fear, but in that moment, I'd never felt so alive.

Tayte's face changed, his eyes hardening, darkening. But there was no censure in his expression. Far from it. The look in his eyes sent desire spiraling right to my core.

"Then what do you want, sweetheart? Tell us."

I want... I want...

I stepped back, needing to look at all three of them. I'd had so many fantasies, detailing loving all three of these men in the strongest, hottest and fiercest of ways.

"I want you all to take me... every way, as much as you want. I want you to hold nothing back."

Tayte, Sam and Dane looked at each other with wide, scared eyes.

They were going to say no, I just knew it!

"Please. I need to feel wanted, desired, lusted after. Please don't make me feel like I'm second class—not good enough. Please."

I began to cry, *damn it.* I dashed away the tears.

"Stupid hormones. Ignore them. Please."

Dane crept forward first. "Tell me what you want, beautiful."

I swallowed.

Oh my God, I never thought I'd have to say this.

But there was only one way to do this, and that was with complete openness and honesty.

"I want to suck your cocks."

Dane was the first to react, his mouth dropping open.

The joke was just sitting there for me to make, and I couldn't resist. I reached up and briefly touched my finger to his lips. "Yes... like that."

He choked on a laugh.

"Um, okay. Where do you want us?"

I glanced at the bed. "Standing against the edge of the bed, please. All three of you."

Dane rushed over to where I pointed, with Sam and Tayte moving more slowly. Then they lined up for me.

Three men.

Three cocks.

I pressed my hand to my mouth, the beauty of the smorgasbord before me overwhelming in the extreme.

And the best part? They were all mine.

I dropped to the floor and crawled over to where they stood, going for Dane's reasonably sized cock first since it was slightly less intimidating than the other two. Only slightly, though.

I knelt before him and stared at it, absurdly feeling like Goldilocks at a feast of a very different kind.

I glanced across at the three men, all at varying degrees of arousal, their large heads and long shafts getting bigger with each man. Dane, then Sam, then finally the largest, Tayte.

I exhaled, my courage deserting me even though I'd been given what I wanted. Served up on a platter.

But I wasn't backing out now. If I gave up, they'd never give me the chance again.

I leaned forward and put my lips around Dane's cock.

He thrust forward, straight into my mouth, and I moaned.

He pulled back, the hard flesh slipping from my lips, and I frowned up at him, not understanding why he'd withdrawn.

"Fuck. I'm sorry, Celeste. Your mouth was way too hot."

I blinked at him. He was apologizing?

"Don't be sorry. Do it again. Teach me what to do."

Dane glanced at Sam and Tayte.

I waited, my heart pounding against my ribs in equal measures of fear and desire—fear of not doing it right, and yet the need building within me at the sensuality of the situation.

"Come on, Dane."

Then he stepped forward and put his hand around the back of my skull, cupping my head.

"Open your mouth."

I did.

And he fed his cock back between my lips.

"Now, suck it, lick it, do whatever you want to it."

His words made my cheeks burn with heat. But I did what he said and explored his rigid flesh.

I came off the end and nibbled down the side, loving his groans as I licked around the bulbous head.

Such an amazing and interesting piece of equipment.

Dane backed away and I shuffled on my knees over to Sam, who was standing, arms by his side and hands clenched into fists.

"Are you okay?" I asked as I knelt before him, looking up at my big man.

His cock seemed ready. It was red and swollen and looked about to explode.

He nodded his head and I bobbed forward, running my tongue up and down the slit and tasting the saltiness of his seed.

I licked my lips, savouring the unusual flavor, before sucking the rest of the head into my mouth.

Sam didn't grab my head, nor did he move. But he trembled beneath my touch and the power of his deliberate submission flooded through me.

He was enjoying this, but I knew he was fighting it for some reason.

I reached up and touched his balls, the soft skin wrinkling and moving up as I caressed him.

He groaned loudly and flexed his hips forward. I swallowed more of the shaft and used my tongue to taste him.

Eventually Sam pulled away, gasping for air.

"Oh, God. That was too good. I can't take any more without coming."

He moved away, as though he couldn't be tempted to even be close to me.

I turned toward Tayte.

Tayte was hard but not yet fully erect, his long cock standing at half-mast, as if he was waiting his turn for arousal.

"Hmmm...." I crawled closer and put my hand around his length, pulling him up to my lips for my treat.

"You don't need to do this, beautiful," he said as he threaded his fingers into my hair.

I could hear it in his words, the warning, the desire to tell me I didn't *have* to go down this path. Not if I didn't want to.

But I wanted this, with everything in me.

I put my mouth over the large head and began to suck.

His grip on my skull tightened as he began to thrust his hips gently.

I moved on him, using his groan and the growing flesh in my

mouth as a guide to what he seemed to want. I pulled my hand up and down the shaft and concentrated on the huge head with my lips and tongue.

He moaned as his cock thickened in my hands, the silky skin stretching over the hard flesh beneath it.

Then, he, too, was pulling away, gripping his cock and pushing it down and away from me.

Why?

To stop himself from coming? If that was the reason, then I'd done a good job.

I got to my feet, my pussy aching and needing them.

I'd never been so aroused in my life, and they hadn't even touched me yet.

"I want all three of you at once. Can you do that?" I looked at Tayte, knowing he'd understand what I was asking.

His face went completely blank for a moment, probably from shock, then a smile began to stretch across his face.

"You really want this, Celeste? To feel all of us inside you?"

I nodded quickly. "Yes, please. I want to know what it feels like to be at the center of the triad, loved by all of you."

Sam let loose a low growl I'd never heard before and Dane came over and hoisted me to my feet. "I need to prepare you first. Lie on the bed."

I considered saying no. After all, I wanted this to be different from every other time.

But I couldn't. Dane's eyes were wild, flames of desire licking at his irises.

And as he pushed me toward the bed and pulled my legs out from under me, I realized he wasn't asking.

I lifted my knees as he knelt on the floor and dove down to place his mouth over my already swollen sex.

"Oh... fu...uck."

I grabbed for his head as he ate my flesh with a ferocity I'd never experienced.

He licked and sucked and flicked my clit until I was gasping for air.

"Enough," Tayte commanded and the pleasure stopped.

I grabbed for Dane's head, needing him back there, working on me. But he was gone.

Then Tayte lay on the bed next to me, obviously close to the edge, judging by the strained look on his face.

"Get on top of me, Celeste."

The Alpha had his legs hanging over the end of the bed and he looked like he'd topple off if he wasn't careful. He was that close to the side edge.

But I did as I was told, trusting my Alpha and what he had in store for me.

He held his cock upright with one hand, the head sticking up, pointing like an arrow at the sky.

I threw my leg over his thighs and settled over him.

I smiled down at Tayte as he looked up at me. What an incredible position to be in.

I tilted my pelvis back until I felt the smooth, hot flesh of him sliding into my core. Then I slowly lowered myself down onto him, feeling him forging deep into me.

I pressed further down, breathing hard as I was filled with the most incredible pleasure. Both physical and emotional.

They all wanted me.

They really did.

I could feel it in the air around me. In the heat of the room. In the barely controlled way the men breathed and panted.

Not to mention the hard cock beneath me, impaling my body.

"That's a girl. Now lean forward."

I put my hands on the bed and leaned as far forward as I could, with my belly resting against Tayte's.

He grinned at me.

"Hello, sweetheart."

"Hello, my love."

I wanted to kiss him, but I couldn't lean forward that far.

Then I felt hands on my back, moving down and opening my ass.

"What...?" I glanced around and there was Sam, slicking up his cock with the lube we used sometimes.

"You wanted to know what it was like to have us all at once? Well, this is it."

I swallowed the lump in my throat as fear of the unknown began to ride me.

Sam pressed his cock to my back package and gently slid in.

Pain pierced me and I moaned, both from the unexpected entry and the pleasure of such a naughty, intense experience.

"Breathe. Focus on me," Tayte said as he tweaked my nipples with his fingers and thrust up into my pussy.

Sam slid in and out gently, going a little deeper each time.

My belly was beginning to tighten, the pleasure over-riding the pain.

I was going to come.

No. Not yet.

"Dane. I need you, too."

My Omega was by the side of the bed, standing next to my head.

Ah... that's why Tayte has us so close to the edge.

"Here you go beautiful. Suck this."

I pulled his cock into my mouth and mere seconds later, my orgasm hit. Being loved by all three of my men at the same time was beyond anything I could ever have imagined.

I moaned around his flesh as my pussy and back passage rippled around the cocks inside me.

Tayte and Sam groaned and gasped as I began to shiver.

My eyes rolled shut and I moaned loudly.

"Oh, damn... Tayte, I'm never going to last," Sam said from behind me.

I came off Dane's cock long enough to say, "Good. Don't last too long, please. This is too much."

I was so full, the feelings of possession and submission so intense.

"Should we stop?" Tayte asked and I wanted to scream at him.

No, this was what I wanted. What I'd asked for. What I craved!

But the reality was far more than I'd expected and my body wasn't going to be able to cope with the pressure much longer.

"Don't you dare! I want you to all come inside me." The crescendo was building again. I couldn't stop the waves of desire rushing up again.

Fuck.

My belly tightened and pushed me over that incredible cliff of pleasure into spasms that fel like they would never end.

Tayte and Sam began to move faster. Tayte thrust up into my pussy, making my clit tingle and throb, while Sam fucked my ass.

I screamed as the next wave of orgasms hit.

I couldn't stop shaking and clenching. I could barely see for the stars exploding in front of my eyes.

I grabbed Dane's cock and pumped it with my hand.

I looked up at him, meeting his gaze. "You too, please. Come with them at the same time."

He nodded, desperate need in his gaze, and guided my head back to his cock.

I sucked on his flesh as deeply as I could, while breathing hard through my nose.

I couldn't handle much more of this.

They were filling me in every way they could. I could feel their love, their desire, their cocks. Their everything.

I came off Dane's flesh to beg. "Please... please..."

Sam began to cry out. "I'm gonna blow."

Oh, thank God for that.

Tayte grabbed my hips and began to fuck me hard.

Fast.

Frantically.

Giving me everything I'd ever wanted.

My eyes closed as my head fell back.

I was surrounded by them, their need, their desire for me.

I pumped Dane's cock with my hand as Sam grabbed my hair, crying out as he came. "Fuuucckkkk!"

He filled me with his hot seed, which set off yet another orgasm, this one even more intense than the previous ones.

I screamed and shook, my whole body milking my men's cocks as they gave me their all.

Tayte went next, growling beneath me and pumping his seed into my pussy. Dane was the last to release and, as I squeezed his shaft with my hand, hard, his cock splashed cum across my breasts in hot, long spurts.

I couldn't see.

I couldn't think.

I could only feel the rolling intensity of giving everything to my triad and receiving all they had in return.

Sam pulled out of my ass and I gasped with the loss of the strange pleasure/pain that he'd inflicted on me.

Dane jumped on the bed and reached for me. I went with him and we all piled onto the pillows, a tangle of arms and legs.

And sperm. Everywhere.

No one spoke.

Instead, the room was filled with frantic, uneven breathing and pounding heartbeats.

I stared up at my men, who looked intensely happy.

Shocked, but happy.

"Next time," I said, and they all looked to me, "can you all swap around so I get to feel you all in different places?"

Dane grinned and Tayte growled.

Sam dropped a kiss on my lips as they all began to laugh. "Oh, yeah, sweetheart," he said. "Anything you want."

EIGHT

TAYTE

he weeks went by and our beautiful mate grew bigger and bigger.

Claire said the baby would arrive in a few short weeks, and although we were excited, we were on tenterhooks waiting for the arrival.

Every day one of us would stay home from work, and if we had no choice but to be away, one of our moms would stay with our waddling, grumpy girl.

She was "done" according to her.

Done with being pregnant, and with being "fat".

We loved her being so big, but only being a hair over five feet tall, it was obvious how uncomfortable she was.

There was a knock at the door. I left Sam with Celeste to answer it.

"Oh, hey, Gray. How are you doing?"

Another great thing about us finding our human mate was the closeness we'd developed between our pack and Grayson's.

Dexter's pack, too.

Having our women had brought us all together.

"I'm good, we're all good. Hey, Celeste. How are you doing?" He waved from the front door and Celeste waved back.

"I'm okay, Grayson. Looking forward to getting this baby out."

He chuckled. "Yeah, Claire is, too."

Grayson dropped his voice. "Can you come outside? I need to fill you in on something."

Sounded serious.

"Yeah, of course." I stepped outside and shut the door. "What's up?"

"The bears are on the hunt. We've had sightings and their scent is everywhere."

The hairs on the back of my neck stood up. They were looking for Celeste.

"Are you sure?"

"Yes. I've gone out myself to check. They've surrounded the pack. The smell of them is everywhere."

I suppressed my shudder. My mate. My baby.

"Do you think this is because of Celeste? Do you think they've seen her? Tracked her here?"

Grayson shrugged. "Don't know, and it doesn't really matter. They've been coming for us since the moment Claire was found." Grayson's jaw clenched and tightened. "And they hid Nevaeh from us for years."

I nodded. "I told the elders what Celeste had told me when she first came to the pack. That the bears believe we're meant to die off. And that Fate wants us to be the last of the wolf shifters."

Which was totally fucked, but what could we do about it?

Grayson crossed his arms over his chest.

"Yeah, we've been talking about that. So, would the bears attack again to grab our women? Even though they knew the humans were our fated mates? Will they try to grab them now they're pregnant? Or will they attack the whole town?"

Tension tightened in my shoulders and I rolled my neck.

"If that happened, a lot of people would die. They've got an extra generation of female shifters, not to mention more numbers in total. We have our mothers, who would want to fight, of course."

I grimaced.

Grayson continued, "There would be chaos. Our fathers would be split between protecting their mates and fighting for the pack. It would be a complete and utter cluster fuck."

I ran my hand through my hair. "We can't let that happen, Gray."

"I know… I know… but what do we do?"

I crossed my arms over my chest.

I had an idea, but how the hell did we mediate it?

"If we could put together a meeting, Alpha to Alpha, between the bears and us, maybe we could establish some rules, a fair fight, something…?"

Grayson nodded. "Yeah, that's an option. Otherwise, we're going to have to go on the offensive and take a hunting party to their den. We can't just sit here and wait for them to attack. We're too vulnerable. The way we have the town set up, it's beautiful, but a whole pack or two could go down, and the rest of the pack at large wouldn't even know."

Fuck.

He was right.

I'd have to ask Celeste for help with this plan.

"I agree. Maybe I can.... Shit, I didn't want to have to do this."

Grayson knew what I was going to say. "Maybe you can ask your mate for some help? She'd know the layout of their den, maybe ask them about the structure of their day? Weaknesses? Anything that could help us?"

I groaned.

Deep down I'd known it would come to this. After the bears had attacked Dexter's pack, then Grayson's. They wouldn't stop until one of our shifter families was dead.

And it wasn't going to be us.

"I'll ask her. I didn't want to put Celeste under this sort of pressure, feeling like she has to betray her own family. But I will."

I'd known we'd need Celeste's help, but I hadn't wanted to ask her. After everything she'd been through, this was additional stress she just didn't need, especially at this time during her pregnancy.

"I'll speak to her and get back to you."

I patted Gray on the shoulder and walked back inside my home.

Celeste was up and making some dinner for us all.

"Can we help you, sweetheart?" I asked, glaring at Sam. He knew she was meant to be resting.

My Beta glared right back. "Don't look at me like that. I tried."

Celeste grunted.

Yep, *grunted*, from the kitchen. "I'm not helpless, Tayte. I know I look like a beached whale, but I've got four weeks to go, so I've gotta keep moving or I'll go crazy. So... spaghetti for dinner?"

She didn't sound like she was asking, and an annoyed vibe was radiating from her now.

"Um, sure, sweetheart. Do you mind if I ask you a few questions while you're doing that?"

She looked toward me while she pulled out the pasta and put some water on to boil.

"Yeah, of course. Sit. Is this something to do with what Grayson came over to discuss with you?"

She wasn't slow, this one.

"Yes. The pack has noticed the scent of bear shifters around town, and we were hoping you could tell us more about the den where you lived."

I kept my voice as soft as possible, but I saw the way my once steady girl began to shake.

"It's okay, sweetheart. You're safe here, with us. I promise."

She dried her hands with a towel. "Yes of course. I know that. It's just... well, the thought of them so near. Even if they were just passing by, or maybe scouting around for info." She shuddered. "What do you want to know?"

"Things like numbers within the den, how many do you think would fight if they all attacked at once?"

I knew it was a hard question to start with, but it was what I most needed to know. What gave us the most concern.

Celeste bit her lip and leaned against the island bench.

"Okay... let me think. Forty-five apartments, times five, at least."

I didn't know what she was calculating but I trusted what she was doing in her head.

She caught my eye and continued. "There's at least two-hundred-and-fifty bear shifters in that den."

"Ah... say what?"

I couldn't believe it. That was twice as many as we had anticipated.

"Not all of them would fight if they attacked here. There're children and lots of elderly, too. But I'd say at least a hundred of strong, fighting age. All shifters. Male and female."

"Whoa."

Now I was surprised they hadn't attacked already.

Celeste smiled at me. "You're wondering why they haven't wiped you guys out already, aren't you?"

I nodded. "Was I that obvious?"

She began to move around the kitchen, getting things out to make a tomato-based pasta sauce.

She grinned like she already knew the answer. "It's because they're lazy, and unorganized, not to mention unfit. To get all of them to attack at one time would be way above their capabilities."

"So, we have the advantage, then?"

She nodded thoughtfully. "Yes. But what for? You're not thinking of attacking first, are you?"

"I honestly don't know, sweetheart, but we can't wait. We're sitting ducks."

We had to improve the security, set up an alarm system.

Something.

We were under attack, or would soon be.

Celeste came around the bench and slid her hands around my neck. "Please be careful, Tayte. You know you're the anchor of this family. We'd all die without you."

I chuckled as I ran my hand over the swollen belly that housed my child.

"Sweetheart, I have more to live for now, than I have ever had in my life."

But I also had more to protect. More to lose than I'd ever had before.

I kissed Celeste and excused myself.

I needed to talk to Dex or one of the elders. I had to give them the information I had, and perhaps set up a meeting for them to talk more with Celeste.

They'd have more questions, and I was sure she could answer them.

I was stepping out the front door when suddenly Dexter arrived, dragging a bleeding Omega with him.

"Dex! Speak of the devil, I was just coming to find you. Who have you got here?"

I didn't like to step into another man's pack and tell him how to do his job, but this Omega needed some protection, obviously. But it wasn't Dexter's Omega, so whose was he?

"We found out who the mole was." Dex spat as he threw the Omega at my feet.

I helped the guy up, but he could only stand on one leg. His left eye was swollen shut and his shoulder looked oddly-shaped. It had clearly been dislocated. The man must be in enormous pain.

"What do you mean?" I asked Dex.

Mole? We had a mole in our pack?

Dex nodded at the bleeding guy. "I mean... we knew there was someone feeding information to the bears. It was the only thing that made sense. How else could they have attacked within a day of us bringing Claire home? Now we know they've been scouting for more information."

I turned on the Omega, who'd obviously been beaten to reveal the information.

"Is this true?"

He ducked his head. "Yes, Alpha."

"But why? Why would you betray us?"

He lifted his gaze and deep in the darkness of his eyes, I saw true hatred. Hatred for us. For his own kind. It disgusted me.

"Because I could. Because they paid me. Why wouldn't I?"

He stuck his chin out in defiance I'd never seen in a pack member, particularly an Omega.

I was tempted to punch him right in the face. To wipe that look off his mouth.

But he'd taken as much beating as he could, and I not the kind of Alpha to beat an Omega half to death.

"What the hell do you mean? You betrayed us! You could have gotten Claire, or any of the others, killed."

He shrugged and looked away. "What do I care? I'll never have a mate like you guys have. I don't even have a triad pack."

He tossed his hair and glared at me with his one remaining good eye. "And thanks to me, you guys probably never will, either. Once they get here."

I grabbed his bad arm and he cried out in pain.

I didn't let go.

"Tell me their plan. Now."

There was movement behind me as my pack surrounded us, but I didn't take my eyes off the Omega.

"Tell me."

I squeezed his arm a little harder. What was a little pain compared to what the bears would bring our way?

"They're going to... ah...."

He swallowed hard, his eyes closing, probably from the pain.

"Tayte. You're hurting him." Celeste drew close to me and the Omega looked at her, his one good eye bulging when he saw how pregnant she was.

I took advantage of that moment. "Is that what you want, Omega? To have Celeste captured? Killed? Because you know that's what's going to happen when the bears arrive."

"The bears? They're coming? I thought they were just, I don't know, scouting around a bit." Celeste gasped and shrunk back.

I couldn't look at my mate to reassure her, because my wolf teeth were bared and I couldn't retract them. I didn't want to scare her even more.

"Omega, you're going to call the bears and set up a meeting with them. I want to work out what the fuck is going on, and you're going to help me."

The Omega, bless his courageous heart, actually threatened me.

"Or what?"

I laughed and gripped tighter to his shoulder. He wanted to know what I'd do to protect my pack?

I pulled his dislocated arm down and twisted until he was kneeling on the dirt screaming at me to stop.

I let go, a little.

"Or I'll rip you apart, piece by piece, I swear it. On the life of my unborn child, Omega. You have no idea what I'd do to keep them both safe."

The Omega nodded and I let him go.

"Okay... I'll call them."

And he did.

The meeting was set.

We just had to work out what they wanted more than our extinction, and figure out how to give it to them.

I convinced my pack to go to bed, to stay safe, while Gray, Dex and I went into the forest to talk to the Alpha of the bear's den.

We didn't have much of a plan, other than to broker a truce.

Somehow.

"If Trevor actually turns up, guys, I swear I'll kill him," Grayson said as we walked up the road and into the clearing where we'd organized to meet.

Not too far from the pack, if we needed back-up.

"You keep your feelings to yourself, Gray," Dex threatened. "We need this to be as impersonal as possible."

Grayson snorted.

I had to laugh. "Impersonal, Dex? Then you should have sent some of the elders to this meeting. It doesn't get much more personal than this for me, you and Gray."

The others grunted in agreement.

Dex nodded. "So, we stick to the plan, and hope to God they haven't brought an army with them."

Grayson said. "If they have, we shift and run. We won't stand a chance of winning out here against a hundred bear shifters."

Dex said, "My pack's on standby, and so is the rest of the town."

We trudged forward and I glanced behind me again.

I had the strangest feeling we were being followed, but every time I looked behind us, I saw nothing.

My heart, which was already beating too hard, began to bang against my ribs.

"Do you smell that?"

The scent of bear was on the breeze, and it suddenly became too strong to stand. A stench.

Why did they never bathe or clean themselves? Disgusting creatures.

I forced myself not to cover my nose, so they didn't see my revulsion if they were around.

And then they were there, in front of us.

Five of them, all big brutes. But at least they were in human form—for now.

I'd half-expected them to bring bodyguards in the shape of their bear shifter forms.

"I see you brought back-up," Dex called out.

The agreement had been for three only.

"Well, you can never trust a wolf to keep his word," the big guy in the middle said, then laughed at his own joke.

I heard Grayson's low growl and stepped closer to him, but didn't say anything.

I didn't know if everyone could keep their cool at this meeting, but doing so was the best chance we had to avoid outright war.

"We kept our word, Trevor. There's three of us. And we're here. How about we get down to business?"

Trevor narrowed his gaze at me. "And what business is that, wolf?"

"I'm Tayte. I'm..."

"I know who you are. You're the guy who knocked up Celeste."

The bears around Trevor growled all of a sudden, the mood within the group changing. The anger ramped up a notch and my wolf threatened to rise up in response.

I took a slow, deep breath.

I needed to play this carefully. Cards close to my chest.

They couldn't know how important Celeste was to me, or we'd all be lost.

Brains over heart, in this case.

"Yeah... that's me. How'd you know?"

"I can smell her on you, even now. That stench we all had to put up with for years. Ugh." He shuddered as though my mate repulsed him and the wolf inside of me howled.

But I pushed him down.

I needed to show Grayson and Dexter how to stay calm, even when the bears baited us.

"Back to the business at hand, Trevor. We know you guys have some sort of plan to attack the pack, and we need to come to an agreement before that happens."

There was a beat of silence.

Yes, that confirmed it.

"Why would I want to do that?" Trevor asked.

I could see his point, but no matter how they played their attack, they'd lose numbers on their side, too.

"Because there's no fight between us. We've done nothing to you, you've done nothing to us. There's no reason we need to fight at all."

And as far as I knew, that was true.

Even the elders couldn't understand why the bears wanted a war with us.

Trevor grunted. "My father believed that you wolf shifters were meant to die out. Become extinct."

I'd heard this from Celeste and was ready for this argument.

"But Fate found a way around it and sent us human mates. Doesn't that say something? That we're not meant to die off?"

Trevor grimaced and I saw a small amount of reasoning come to life in his eyes.

"There are a lot of people who believe what my father believed. That you all should be left to rot. And after Celeste betrayed us, then ran off, my den wants revenge. They want to attack."

I paused. He didn't want this. Nevaeh had told me once that Trevor's father had forced him to date her. Surely, he'd want to just walk away?

And I could work with that.

I smiled calmly. "But if you don't want to risk your den by attacking us, surely you, as the Alpha, must be followed."

Trevor was nodding and I could almost hear the cogs in his brain clicking around. "I may be able to hold them off until a treaty can be organised, but you need to give us something in return."

Anything.

"What do you want? Supplies? Cash?"

"We want Celeste back."

Cold dread skittled down my spine. I had expected that, but hearing it out loud made the threat against my mate seem more real. "Why?"

I already knew. They wanted to kill her. Punish her. I could tell.

Trevor looked amongst his den mates, puffing up his chest like a dickhead.

"She was sentenced to death by me, and the sentence must be carried out. It'll be the only way to appease my den, maintain order. A sacrifice for the greater good. Surely you'd do that."

I didn't move, or speak, I couldn't.

And the Alphas alongside me weren't helping.

They knew my struggle and would never sacrifice their own mates for the good of the overall pack.

"You want me to send her back to you so you can kill her?" I had to repeat his words back to him, just so I was one-hundred percent sure what he was saying.

And I had to hold my temper.

Dexter and Grayson and I had sworn to each other not to show our cards.

Not to declare the importance of our fated mates in our lives, as Celeste had confirmed that the bears didn't have such mates.

And he showed me she'd been correct when he said, "You can get another mate. Women are interchangeable."

I nodded and cleared my throat, working out what to say. I had to buy us some time to work out a new plan. Because I was never giving her up. I would die first.

"I agree... women are interchangeable."

The lie tasted like ash on my tongue.

Dexter turned to me and shook his head in the smallest of gestures, but I focused on Trevor, a plan forming in my mind.

"You know our pack is childless, woman-less."

"Yes." He grinned and exchanged satisfied looks with his den mates.

I wanted to squash their arrogance with my fist. But I pushed down my anger.

"Then give me four more weeks. After that, I'll hand Celeste over to you and you can do with her as you will."

There was the faintest gasp, a whisper on the wind that tugged at my attention, but I couldn't focus on it.

This was too important. I had to buy us time, so I could save our pack.

"What will four weeks change?" Trevor asked.

"I told you, our pack is childless, and she's pregnant with my baby. Let me get my kid from her first. It's only a few short weeks away, then you can have her."

Oh my God, my heart actually hurt to say the words.

Never!

"You'll surrender her to me?"

Like hell I will.

"Of course, once I've got my baby you can have the human."

My wolf screamed inside my mind. Howled like a crazy at the moon. But I wasn't stopping this line of argument. Not now that I'd started along this path.

It gave us time, and it showed the pack how crazy the bears truly were.

"Okay, then we can talk about a treaty. My father is gone, and honestly, I just want to get on with our lives. Though... I've seen your houses and I want one like that. We don't have what you do."

That's because you're fucking lazy!

"We're all tradesmen; we can help you with everything. Let me go back to the elders to work out a deal."

Like hell we'll work for free for these guys.

"Fine, wolf. You get your four weeks. Then we're coming for the little slut."

I nodded as if I agreed with his statement, though I wanted to reach out and close my hand around his neck. Squeeze hard until the life left him and he fell to the ground at my feet.

How dare the bastard threaten my mate? My true love?

I swallowed rage, and then we retreated.

We had to get back to the pack.

The smell on the breeze as we turned away from the bears was strangely familiar.

What was it...?

"What the fuck was that?" Dex spat at me, finally speaking.

My wolf was practically bursting through my skin.

"Calm your farm, Dex."

I began to strip and so did the other two, the energy between us burning angry and bright. No way could I stay in human form with this much adrenaline rushing through me.

"I bought us time. Nothing else. Those bears are gonna die."

My wolf ripped through my body, my human side unable to stay in control with the rage that filled me boiling through my blood.

We ran back to the pack as quickly as we could, around the forest that protected our families.

There didn't seem like a way around this war now. We'd have to fight.

Because there was no way they were *ever* getting my mate.

NINE

CELESTE

Bile rose in my throat and I choked on it. Tayte wanted to hand me over to the bears?

I couldn't let them hear me; I couldn't.

So, I swallowed the acid, and the tears.

I had to get out of here.

I crept away and began to run, stumbling over tree roots, long grass and thick shrubs. My belly was so cumbersome, but I carried myself the best I could as I cut across the forest. Away from the bears, and more importantly, away from the pack I had thought was my family.

They were going to kill me!

The bears for honor, and the pack to save their own hides.

What had I done to deserve all this?

Be born human.

The tears ran down uncontrollably down my face as my baby rolled and kicked within my womb. It was as if the child sensed its mother's anguish.

I had to get away from here.

Those wolves were not going to take my baby from me.

And they were certainly not going to send me back to the den for my *punishment.*

Anger pushed me harder. I ran, tripping and stumbling, through the forest.

But I didn't stop, though the cold ate at my skin and the pain in my heart made me want to cry.

I have no idea how long I ran. My legs trembled and my whole body shivered with fear and the pain of rejection.

I turned back my head to look over my shoulder. Had any of them heard me, when I inadvertently let out that gasp? What if they'd heard me?

I face the front again, and took another step forward, and then I was falling, slipping down a hill I hadn't noticed.

And the world went black.

Sam

I woke to a cold hand on my shoulder, shaking me awake. It was Tayte, and by the look of him, he'd only just returned from a run.

"Hey, where's Celeste?" Tayte said. There was an urgency to his voice that had me sitting up.

I glanced to the other side of the bed, where I'd left her.

She was always surrounded by pillows these days, and didn't like us getting too close in sleep. She got too hot and her back hurt, so we had temporarily given her some space.

But the place that should have housed my mate was empty.

"I don't know. Where's Dane? Maybe she's with him?" But as I said the words, cold fear spread through my gut. That tone of Tayte's had not been conducive to low stress. "What's wrong?"

"She's gone. I can't find her. Dane's getting dressed. Get up, get some clothes on."

I pulled on some jeans and a sweatshirt as quickly as I could, though it was pointless. I could feel my wolf stir and Tayte's speech was a little garbled as he struggled to talk through his shifter teeth.

Our clothes would be shredded soon if the mood continued like this.

"What's going on, Tayte?"

I followed him down the stairs and Dane met us in the living room.

"Where's Celeste?" Dane asked.

My brain was empty, free of all thoughts, as my shock rammed into me. "She's eight months pregnant; where the hell could she have gone?"

The front door opened and Dexter walked in. "She's not at my place and Claire hasn't seen her."

Tayte's fingers tightened into fists. "Fuck! I knew it. I felt her —I even caught her beautiful scent—but I thought I was imagining it. This is all my fault."

I grabbed my Alpha's arm and shook him. "What the hell are you talking about?"

He sighed heavily, running his hands through his hair.

"I... ah, I think Celeste followed me into the woods tonight."

"Why would she do that?"

Tayte shrugged. "Maybe she was worried about us? Maybe she wanted to help? I have no idea, but I heard a few noises as we walked into the forest and thought we may have been followed. But I dismissed the idea, because who would be that stupid?"

Good point, but dear God, she could be anywhere.

I groaned. "Okay... fine. Where is she? We need to find her."

Tayte grimaced. "We do. But you need to know something before we go. If she heard what I said to the bears, then she'll be running away from us."

"But... why would she do that?" I grabbed him by the shirt. "What did you say?"

I could barely talk now.

My teeth were shifting, and my eyes had flashed to wolf's night vision.

I could only see in black and white, though a red haze was covering me.

Tayte sighed, not looking at me. "I told the bears they could have her once the baby was born."

I pulled back my arm and punched my Alpha as hard as I could.

Pain cracked through my wrist as Tayte reeled back, blood dripping from his nose.

"If something's happened to her or that baby, Tayte..." I panted and began to strip.

She was in danger. I could feel it. And it was all *his* fault.

I let my wolf tear through me. My black Beta wolf that was almost as big as my Alpha. Today, I would take him down if I needed to.

I ran straight out the door and put my nose into the air.

Blood. My mate's blood.

Oh, fuck, no.

I began to run, the other wolves behind me.

They were on my tail, but I ran faster.

How could he do this to us?

To her?

After everything she'd been through.

I pushed down my anger, the feelings consuming me and making me want to turn around and fight my own pack.

But my mate needed me. That was more important now.

I'd deal with the guilt later.

The scent of her sweetness, her blood, made me turn off the road and into the forest.

She'd come this way. I could smell her. Frightened and bleeding.

I skittered all the way to the edge of a cliff and looked down.

All my nightmares came true in that one moment when I stared down to the bottom of the cliff.

Celeste's broken body lay in a tangle of brush. Her blonde hair was strewn over a fallen tree branch.

I threw back my head and howled, alerting my brothers to the pain I was in and letting loose the raging feelings bottling up in my head.

Then I ran, making my way down the cliff as fast as I could, slipping and sliding on the loose dirt, the rocks cutting my paws.

Oh my God, she's dead.

She's dead.

The baby... please no.

I hit the ground and put my nose against my mate, my heart pounding in my chest as I checked to see if she was alive.

If I felt her dead, cold skin against my nose I didn't know what I'd do.

Kill Tayte would likely be first on the list.

But she moved. She moaned.

She rolled her head and I let go of my wolf so fast, my human skin hurt as it stretched back to fit me.

"Ah... fuck..."

My head spun with the speed of my shift, but I put my fingers to her neck, feeling a pulse.

I looked up, where my pack and Dexter's wolves stood on top of the cliff.

I called out to them. "She's alive! You need to get Claire! And an ambulance!"

Dexter and his pack took off and Tayte howled.

I knew he wanted to come down also, but I didn't want to deal with the Alpha at this moment.

"Find a safe way down for Claire."

I squatted next to my mate, wishing for blankets and towels and an air lift.

I cradled her face gently, careful not to disturb her neck.

She could have broken anything.

Or everything.

Then her eyes opened, slowly, and she began to cry.

"Sam.... the baby, the baby's coming. I'm bleeding."

I looked down and realized there was blood over her jeans.

A lot of it.

That's what I'd smelt.

That's how I'd found her.

How horrific.

I'd tracked my mate, because she was bleeding out.

I cupped her face. "Just hold on, Celeste. Hold on. Help's coming."

She tried to sit up, but I pushed her shoulders gently. "No. Please, don't get up, beautiful."

"Tayte... he's going to send me away. The baby..."

I let loose a growl I'd never made. "He will never send you away. Do you understand me? I'll kill that bastard first. You will live with us, and give us more babies forever, do you understand me?"

I was crying now, and I couldn't stop.

"Celeste! Celeste!"

She closed her eyes and she wasn't waking up this time.

Oh my God, what do I do?

There was noise above and around me.

I wanted to drag my mate close and hold her.

But I was too scared to damage her, and knew that I couldn't do anything.

I just stood next to her almost-lifeless body, doing nothing. Feeling useless.

"Help me! Please!"

Claire was suddenly there next to me, with a bag and blankets.

"Move out of the way, Sam. The paramedics are on the way."

Claire checked Celeste's pulse and the baby's heartbeat with a stethoscope.

"They're both alive."

"But... the blood." I gestured to the blood staining Celeste's thighs. "Surely the baby can't survive this."

"Cover her up. Quick. Keep her warm."

I followed Claire's orders.

"Claire, tell me. What are her chances of surviving this?"

Claire's face was grim, her lips twisted as she considered how to answer me.

"I don't know what her injuries are. If she's fractured her spine, or has massive internal bleeding, she'll be in for a big struggle."

"And the baby?"

"The bleeding is probably an indication of a placental abruption, so the baby is still alive. But we need to get her to the hospital for a C-section as soon as possible."

"How long do they have?" I asked.

Claire shook her head. "I don't know, Sam. I honestly don't know. But we need to get her to hospital. Now."

I could hear sirens.

I didn't know how much time had passed but Celeste was getting paler by the minute.

Claire glanced behind her. "Oh, thank God, they're here. Tayte's gonna bring them down, but we may need to help them through the brush. This isn't an easy spot to get to."

I growled, loudly. "You get Tayte away from her, or I'll kill him. This is all his fault."

"Sam..."

"Claire, I'm serious."

"Fine. I'll go get the paramedics."

Claire disappeared and someone called out to me.

I looked up and Dane was throwing down a pair of rolled up jeans. They snagged on a tree, then fell down in the dirt.

I hadn't even considered my own nakedness. I grabbed them and pulled them on.

That would have been fun to explain to the humans, why I

was naked and in the middle of the forest with an unconscious woman.

It was going to be hard enough as it was.

"Here she is."

Two men with a stretcher hurried over and Claire pulled me out of the way.

"She's thirty-six weeks pregnant and bleeding. We'll need to prep the OR for an emergency C-section as soon as we get back."

The men tied Celeste to the white stretcher and carried her off to an ambulance.

"I'll ride with her," Claire said to me. "Get your car and drive to the hospital. I'll meet you there."

I nodded.

I didn't want to let Claire take her, but there was nothing more I could do. And there was no extra room in the back of that tiny ambulance with her. I could see that.

So, I trusted Dexter's mate to take care of Celeste.

I had to. Because my own pack had sure as shit let her down.

As the ambulance drove off, I was left with a sinking, horrible feeling. One of pure grief and despair.

I'd never recover from this if Celeste and her baby died.

Tayte was suddenly next to me and I was no longer alone with my feelings. Instead, my need to hurt him was pure and nasty, and bigger than me.

I looked at him and spat. "If she dies, you're dead."

Tayte nodded. "I know. Because I won't be able to live without her."

His grief came at me in a wave. I couldn't handle it. What he carried was too much for me now.

Grief *and* regret.

"No."

I let go of my human self and shifted back to my wolf, and I started running home.

I needed my clothes. I needed my car and I needed my mate.

Our baby's life hung in the balance, and my family was in tatters.

What the hell could go wrong next?

TEN

CELESTE

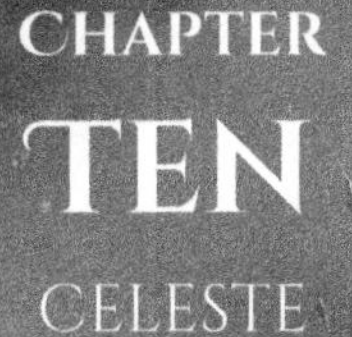

Waking up was harder than it had ever been.

What was wrong with my eyes?

My arms?

My body?

I licked my lips and swallowed the cotton wool feeling in my mouth.

"Celeste? Hello?"

I knew that voice.

It was Dane, I was sure of it.

I blinked, and blinked, and blinked, until my eyes finally opened.

Bright lights shone down on me.

"Where am I?"

Dane was there, gripping my hand. "You're at the hospital."

Hospital? Why would I be at the hospital?

I reached for my belly with my free hand and the baby swelling was gone.

My eyes popped open and I looked down on my now flat-ish stomach. "The baby... my baby?" My voice rose, almost hysterical. "Where is it?"

Dane cupped my face and forced me to look at him.

"She's out and she's doing well. A little premature, and on oxygen in the ICU for a few more days, but she's strong. Just like her mama."

Tears pricked my eyes and I struggled to sit up.

Dane picked up a control and pushed a button. The bed lifted me up until I was almost sitting.

I winced as pain shot through my ribs and I let my head rest back against the pillows.

"She? I had a girl."

I'd always wanted a girl.

Of course, I would have been happy with a boy, with twins. A puppy, even. But a baby girl was the true fantasy.

"Yes, you did, my love. And she's beautiful. Sam's watching over her as we speak."

"What happened?" I didn't remember much at all. "Why am I here?"

Dane pulled up a chair and sat next to me, gripping my hand like he'd never let go.

"You ran away, into the forest, and fell down a cliff embankment. We thought we were going to lose you both, but you were very lucky. You've got a cracked rib or two and some cuts and bruising, but considering how far you fell, we're all thanking our lucky stars that you got away from it so unscathed."

Cracked ribs? I looked down at my hand where a drip was inserted, probably with some very good painkillers too.

"Why would I run away from you all?"

Then the memories came flooding back and I gasped, pulling my hand from Dane's grip.

"You're going to give me to the bears! You don't even want me."

I began to scream. "Help! Somebody! Help me!"

Dane grabbed for my hands again.

I pushed at him, my heart pounding against my ribs. "No! Get away from me! I want my baby! Give me my baby!"

Two nurses and Claire came rushing in. "Celeste, calm down. Please."

I grabbed for Claire's arm and held her tight. "They're going to send me back to the bears; you need to protect me, please. My baby, I need my baby. They're going to steal her from me."

Claire grabbed my hands and squeezed hard.

"Celeste, listen to me. Okay? Listen. No one is taking your baby away. She's in a crib, in the NICU. I can bring her to you, but you can't hold her yet, okay?"

I nodded but couldn't stop shaking.

Claire tried to move away but I grabbed her arm tighter.

"Claire, you can't leave. Tayte said he was going to hand me over to the bears once the baby came. If she's here, then he'll throw me away."

My throat closed up as the betrayal truly hit home.

After giving myself entirely over to them, they were going to get rid of me. After I'd finally let down my guard, let myself believe that they loved me.

A sob rose and I couldn't hold it in.

Claire grabbed for me again. "I'm not going anywhere until we figure all this out, okay? Nurse Myers, could you bring Celeste's baby to us, please?"

I watched the woman go and relaxed a fraction. But I wasn't letting Claire's hand go. No way.

Dane was still in the room, and I shot him a glare before looking back at the doctor.

"They're going to kill me."

I'd known it was all too good to be true.

The wolves had been waiting for me to grow them a baby, and then they were done with me.

The nurse came back into the room, wheeling a clear-sided box with a baby inside.

She was barely dressed and so beautiful my heart broke in half, only to fill up with a love I'd never known existed.

"Oh my God." I let go of Claire's hands and reached for the box. "She'll be cold like that, won't she?"

The baby turned toward my voice and blinked up at me with huge blue eyes.

Oh my God. She's here.

"Hello, baby, I'm your mama. I can't believe I missed your birth." I looked at Claire. "How many days has it been?"

Claire came close and smiled. "She's not cold, don't worry. These humidicribs are kept at a constant ninety-seven degrees, so she's nice and warm. And she was born only twenty-four hours ago. You haven't missed much at all, Mama."

Claire glanced at the door, but I didn't want to take my eyes off my baby.

"Now, you can touch her through these special little sleeves," Claire opened up an access point for me.

I placed my hand inside and reached for my baby. I touched her soft skin on her arm and her tiny little hand.

Her fingers wrapped around my finger and I began to cry, tears slipping down my cheeks.

"How long will she need to stay in here, Claire?"

I'd been four weeks from my due date. How dangerous was that for my baby girl?

"Just a few more days, I think, Celeste. We'll reassess her each day. Now, I'm going to leave her here with you and I'm going to deal with something in the corridor. Just yell if you need me."

"Okay."

I was never going to need anything else, ever again.

I had my little angel.

She'd survived that horrible fall.

We both had.

And now I had to work out a way to survive the next fifty years of my life, because there was no way I was letting the wolves use me as a sacrifice now.

It was four o'clock in the morning when Celeste woke up. A single day had passed since that nightmare of her falling down the cliff.

Sam still wouldn't talk to me and Dane moped around like a puppy with a broken tail.

Our family was falling apart, and somehow, I knew it was all my fault.

Then the door to her hospital room flew open and an angry doctor came at us.

"What the hell is she talking about?" Claire hissed at us.

Oh, fuck.

My fears had come true and poor Celeste had remembered immediately why she'd run from us.

I sighed. "It's my fault, Claire. Ask Dexter about it, he was there. He'll explain everything."

Claire narrowed her eyes and poked me in the chest with her pointed finger.

"You are going to tell me right now what the hell is going on. What was that girl doing at the bottom of a cliff in the middle of the night?"

Claire was practically panting, she was so angry.

I let my shoulders drop, the weight of my guilt too heavy to bear.

"When Grayson, Dexter and I met with the bears, they told us an attack was imminent, and from what Celeste had told me about their numbers, I knew that much of our town would die if it came to war. So, I asked them for a treaty, a way to buy us some time to work out a full solution."

Claire put her hands on her hips. "Okay. So, what did you offer them?"

I glanced over at Dane, who met my look and then grimaced.

I turned back to the doctor who'd saved my child's life.

"They wanted Celeste, so they could carry out the death sentence they'd imposed on her six months ago."

Her mouth dropped open. "You didn't say yes?"

I ran a hand through my hair and tugged at my shirt.

"I had no choice. It was the only thing I could say to put them off attacking. I told them to give me a month, until the baby was born, and then I'd send her back to them."

Claire glared at me with the fury of a thousand suns. "Tell me you're joking."

Why didn't anyone understand that I'd been lying through my teeth? As if I'd *ever* give up my mate. The one person who completed me.

"I would never have done it, ever. You weren't there, ask Dexter. I was in an impossible situation, so I lied. It was just to buy us some time, so we could come up with a plan."

Claire rolled her eyes in a dramatic fashion.

"Oh. My. God. Please tell me she didn't *hear* you lying to the bears."

Dane nodded. "She did, we think. Because she snuck out in the middle of the night and ran off. Nothing else makes sense."

Claire sighed. "She definitely heard you because she was just telling me that you're going to send her back to the bears. Jeezuus... That poor girl."

Claire slapped her palm against her forehead. "What a mess."

My chest cracked open, pain pouring into my wounds like salt.

"I know. What do I do, Claire? How do I explain to her that I was never going to go through with it? That I was saying it to save the pack and give us time to come up with an alternative?"

I clenched my teeth against the wave of nausea that rolled through me.

I'd been sick to my stomach every single moment since this had happened.

Not only did I have to find a way to save my pack and the lives of those in our town, but my mate was hurt and no longer trusted me.

More than that, she thought I was actively involved in wanting to have her killed.

The walls were tumbling down around me and I didn't know what to do.

"What should I do, Claire?"

"You need to explain, apologize and beg forgiveness."

"I know. And I will. But I don't want to upset her any further."

Claire nodded, her phone beeping.

She pulled her cell out of her pocket then sighed. "I'm going to make a phone call, then come back. You three wait out here and I'll be back in a few minutes."

Claire walked off and began talking on her cell.

Sam and Dane sat in the plastic chairs in the hallway and I loitered around, doing laps on the linoleum.

When Claire came back, she had a grim look of determination on her face.

"Okay. Let's go. Tayte, you're with me."

I followed Claire into the hospital room where my mate was talking to our baby through a little incubator box.

I hung by the doorway, ready for the attack.

Claire moved over to her patient. "Celeste, I just spoke to Dex about the other night to confirm what Tayte said about his conversation with the bears."

Celeste pulled her arm out of the incubator and turned to me.

I inhaled sharply when I saw her face. Her anger sliced through my heart like claws through flesh.

"Get him out of here."

I looked toward Claire, who took over.

"Celeste, you need to hear him out. Your whole future, and that of all the packs in the Woodlands depends on it."

That seemed to give Celeste pause, because she drooped, her shoulders sagging as she crossed her arms over her chest.

"Fine. Talk."

"I know you heard what I said to the bears about giving you up after the baby was born. But I would never do that."

She glared at me, her face not changing a single bit.

"I don't believe you."

I laughed sadly. "Well, that's ironic, because I was lying to them, not you. How could you think, after all the love we've shared over the past six months, that I'd ever abandon you?"

She looked away, but I could see the pain in her face.

I went down on my knees to beg.

"Sweetheart, look at me, please. I lied that night. Lied my ass off. You heard me tell them that you weren't my mate, and you know that's a lie. I had to buy us more time. You told me that they outnumber us two to one. My whole town will die if the bears attack as one force. I had to tell them something to give us enough time to mount a proper defence. I will never, ever give you up. Even if you and Sam and Dane vote to kick me out forever, I'll sleep on the doorstep for the rest of my life. To make sure the three of you remain safe. The three of you... and the baby."

She looked at me this time, her blue eyes as dark as granite.

"I know you want the baby... you don't want me."

I shook my head. "You're right about one thing, and horribly wrong about the other. Of course, I want the baby. She's ours, she's yours. But I want *you* even more. How can I prove it to you?"

I stayed on my knees, hoping she'd see how truly sorry I was.

She sighed, but her arms didn't uncross.

"I don't think I'll ever forgive you for what you said that night. I'll never be able to let my guard down with you again. I'll never believe you again when you say that you love me. It's all just... broken. We can't go back."

Hot tears were in my eyes, then on my cheeks.

I dashed them away and looked at the floor.

"Um... okay. I understand."

I got to my feet and backed up to the door.

"I'll move my things out of the house, and you can come home with Sam and Dane. Neither of them forgives me either, so it's probably best that you three stay together."

I moved to walk away, and Celeste called out. "What did you mean, the pack was in danger?"

I turned back to face her. "The bears want blood. Mine, yours, they don't care. They want our pack extinct, gone. So, we either need to change their minds, or we need to fight them."

"Oh, so I was going to be a sacrifice for peace. How noble of you."

Her tone was hard, unforgiving, and the darkness of my guilt consumed me.

"You have it all wrong, sweetheart, as Dexter and Grayson can attest. I lied to the bears to give us a few weeks to plan. Nothing more. I'd rather die than ever see you hurt."

She didn't answer me, only turned back to face her baby once again.

There was only one way forward and that was to eliminate the bears once and for all.

"I love you, Celeste. With all my heart."

She didn't look my way again, but it didn't matter. I was able to say the only words I wanted her to hear. Then I left.

I left the hospital, and I left my pack.

The bears wanted blood, so I'd give it to them.

TWELVE

I watched my Alpha walk out of the hospital and for some reason, I had the most horrible suspicion I'd never see him again.

"I think we need to go speak to Celeste now."

I stood up and walked into the hospital room with Dane.

Then I stopped.

My heart filled.

I couldn't believe how beautiful she was, sitting there with our baby within arm's reach.

"Celeste." I went straight to her hospital bed and tried to gather her into my arms. "You're awake. Please, never leave us again. We love you too much to go through that fear again."

She laughed as she put her head on my chest. "Put you through it? What about me? I missed out on my daughter's birth and seemed to have toppled off a cliff."

I kissed her upturned face. Her button nose. Her forehead. Her pale pink lips.

"You did. And you survived it all. My perfect, brave, strong girl."

I cuddled her close and sighed. "This feels so good. I didn't realize how much I'd miss you until I didn't have you for a day."

She laughed again and pulled away. "So, you weren't part of the plan to toss me away as soon as the baby was born?"

I frowned at her. "Of course not. There's never been such a plan, and there never will be. You're our fated mate, and no one's taking you away from us."

Celeste screwed up her face. "That's not what I heard the other night."

I grimaced. "Yeah, I know. I still can't believe how stupid Tayte was to try and bullshit his way through that meeting."

Celeste blinked up at me. "So, he really was lying?"

"Of course, he was! Are you serious right now?"

Celeste chewed on her bottom lip.

"Tayte said he's going to move out. I'm not sure where he'd go but..."

I gaped at our mate. "He what?"

Celeste's eyebrows rose on her forehead. "I don't think it's a bad idea, actually. We don't need him and I can't forgive him for what he did. He betrayed me."

I reeled backwards, feeling like Celeste had smacked me with an open palm. "Don't need him? Don't *need* him? He's our Alpha. He's the one who holds our family together. Who will save our pack if it comes to a fight?"

Celeste's gaze dropped away and she began playing with her hair, twirling it around her finger and staring at the strands. "Well, you can do that, too."

Now I wanted to shake her.

Sure, Tayte had been stupid and we all wanted to punish him for the consequences of his actions, but she didn't get it.

"I can, but you're not understanding the difference between an Alpha and a Beta."

Celeste shrugged and I began to panic. Tayte looked after us. Guarded us. Would die for us. He was the glue that kept this family together.

"Look. I know what he said was dumb and foolish, and resulted in us almost losing you and our baby. I haven't spoken to him since that night and I was planning on punishing him for a while yet. But breaking up our family... that's a different thing altogether."

I didn't want to lose our pack. It wouldn't function without him.

"I need to find him. He can do his penance another way."

I ran out of the room and along the corridor.

He couldn't have gotten far.

I made my way outside and sniffed the air. Nope. Nothing.

I jogged over to the car park and went up to level three where we'd parked the car.

The truck was still there, and next to it was Tayte's car.

He hadn't taken it, so where was he?

I jogged back down the stairs and went to the cafeteria.

It was five in the morning and no one was around, but I'd been hoping Tayte had come to get a stale coffee, or some food from one of the vending machines.

But there was nothing.

No sign of him.

I walked back to Celeste's hospital room slowly, sniffing the air as I went and not coming up with anything from my Alpha.

When I arrived back at the room, I took a big, careful breath, then informed my Omega and our mate that he was gone.

Dane gaped at me. "What do you mean, he's gone? Gone where?"

Celeste sighed. "What does it matter? Won't he be fine, wherever he is?"

I turned on her and growled. "You don't understand. Tayte has lost his pack, his mate and his baby, or so he thinks. And he has a bear den who wants your blood. How do you think he's going to solve that problem?"

Celeste's eyes began to widen and then her mouth dropped open.

"He wouldn't..." She licked her lips, "He wouldn't do anything stupid, would he?"

My heart was pounding like a runaway train.

"He's going to sacrifice himself to the bears, I just know it," I said.

"But how... why?"

I growled at her again and she paled. "Celeste, you aren't getting it. Tayte is an Alpha. He lives only for his pack. If he believes it will keep you safe, keep all of us safe, he'd sacrifice himself a hundred times over. If those bears want someone's head, then he'll go serve it up on a silver platter."

Oh fuck.

What had I done?

I'd been angry with Tayte... so angry that he'd put Celeste's life in danger. But I never wanted this.

"But he can't... I mean..." She swallowed hard, her eyes turning glossy from unshed tears.

I groaned, feeling frustrated and impotent. Just like I had last night when Celeste's life was fading away before me.

Now it was Tayte whose life could end soon.

"I know you're still mad at him and you can't forgive him for lying about such an important thing, but you need to think. What if it was you? What would you do for someone you truly loved? Our daughter. What level would you stoop to? What lie would you tell? Would you die for her?"

Silvery tears slipped down Celeste's cheeks. "I'd do anything to keep her safe."

I nodded once, feeling the strange calm of an impending battle descend over me. "Then you have your answer as to why Tayte did what he did, and now why he's gone to sacrifice himself."

Celeste let out a sob and I turned away.

"I need to leave. I'm not losing Tayte. Not today."

Celeste grabbed for my hand as I tried to walk away. "What can I do?"

I squeezed her hand. "You can keep our baby safe and get better. Because you are the only thing that matters to us."

"I..." Celeste swallowed, "I didn't realize he would..."

I cupped her face, willing some courage into her.

"None of us did. But you need to remember that we grew up knowing about the fated mate bond and you didn't. You don't understand it the way we do. It is love at first sight, in every way for us. We would die for you. And our daughter."

She sobbed loudly this time, more tears flowing down her cheeks. "I'd rather you lived for us."

I pressed a kiss to her lips. "I'll bring him back."

"Dane, let's go."

We started running and I got on the horn to Dexter and the elders.

It was an hour's drive from the pack to town. Forty-five minutes if they broke every speed limit along the way.

I prayed to God that wouldn't be too late.

We needed to save our Alpha from doing something we were all going to regret.

THIRTEEN

Finding the bear's headquarters was easy enough. I just followed the stench and the information that I'd accumulated from Celeste about them.

She'd told me that they were on the furthest outskirts of town, in a ramshackle apartment block that looked like it was barely holding itself together.

I stared up at the building I'd found in my walking quest.

Celeste had lived here her whole life?

How had she survived?

There were beer cans and cigarette butts littering the grass and not much else around.

It was still early, maybe seven o'clock in the morning.

The humans in the surrounding neighborhood had stirred. Some were on their way to work, school, or whatever else they did.

But the bears didn't seem to have woken yet.

I walked forward, up the path to the apartment block.

Surely, they'd wake up for this? An Alpha wolf coming to surrender?

I lifted my hand and knocked on the door. I waited for a while, then did it again.

What time did these creatures rise? Or more rightly, what time did they go to bed?

Eventually the door opened. A sleepy-looking woman in her twenties or thirties blinked up at me.

"I'm here to see your Alpha."

She yawned at me. "He won't be awake for a while."

Geez, you'd think this sort of thing happened every day.

"It's important. I'll wait."

"Suit yourself."

She showed me inside to a living area, where there was a rundown snooker table and a leather couch with a great big hole in it.

"You may be waiting a while."

So much for charging to my death.

"No problem."

I sat on the couch, avoiding the hole and feeling a strange buzz in my veins. A weird desire to chuckle and laugh aloud overtook me. There was no anger or regret, only warm feelings I couldn't identify.

I'd once read that some people experienced a sort of euphoria before they died. This was what they must have meant.

I chuckled to myself, realizing how ridiculous I sounded even inside my own head.

I waited what felt like hours, but it probably wasn't that long until a young kid stumbled into the room.

He saw me and stopped short. "Who are you?"

He smelled like the wrong end of a horse, and unfortunately my wolf-like senses made me cringe.

"I'm Tayte. Can you get the Alpha for me?"

"Hmm. Okay."

And he wandered off.

Oh my God. Why was I so worried about an attack from these people?

They were unclean, unorganized and slept all day.

But then I heard it.

The rumble of the bears.

The hairs on the back of my neck tingled as a dozen men stepped into the room.

Trevor, their Alpha, was in the center of a the large group.

Celeste was right about their physicality. They were soft bodied and unshaven, and on the surface looked unfit. But they were big, and like the bears they shifted into, I knew they would be fast and strong and mean.

"What the hell are you doing here? I thought you said a month?"

Oh, so they'd partied and relaxed, had they? Thinking they had time before they had to do anything with us.

Maybe I should have come back with a hunting party. Every Alpha and Beta in our pack could have taken these guys down.

But my pack didn't want me. My Beta wouldn't even look at me and my mate had rejected me.

Why would I risk the lives of anyone else, when a simple sacrifice was all these bears wanted?

I squared my shoulders and said what I'd come to say. "I've come to take her place."

Trevor blinked, then glanced to the men at his side, who seemed equally confused.

"What do you mean?"

"I mean exactly what I said. You want Celeste here, so you can carry out your sentence. I'm here to take her place. A peace offering to stop all the fighting."

The men gaped at me.

"But... but... you're an Alpha. You can't do that," Trevor said.

One of the beefy old guys at his side, said, "This is a trap. I'm sure of it."

I wanted to laugh. Why was this so hard for them to believe? Celeste was my *mate*. Of course, I would do anything to save her. Did they not know that?

"Look, this is a simple trade, with one condition. That you swear off attacking the wolf pack and worrying about if they have their mates or not. That was your father's agenda, wasn't it, Trevor?"

The bear shifter lifted his chin in the air. "Yeah. So what?"

"So, you had to date Nevaeh for how long because of all that crap? You lost years when you should have just been here, in your den, with your woman."

Woman? Women?

I didn't know the terminology. And although I'd love to smash Trevor's face in for what he'd done to Nevaeh in the years he'd been with her, this was a negotiation. I had to keep my cool.

"We can't do that," one of the younger guys said.

Trevor looked torn, so I kept talking, hoping to sway him.

"Hey, look. I'm handing myself over to you. If you want to show the den how strong you are, just destroy me. I won't fight you. That'll be enough. And you can leave the rest of the pack alone."

My brain searched for another argument. I hadn't really thought the bears would need convincing, but then it came to me.

"Leave them to their human mates. The wolves will never be as strong as you when the next generation comes through. Those kids might not even be able to shift!"

I had no idea if my daughter would be able to shift or not, but I didn't care. She was perfect and beautiful.

But I was betting the bears would care.

There was a rumble of ascent.

Trevor began to laugh. "That would be an even greater victory, wouldn't it? To see that pack turned into a group of humans!"

He practically rolled on the ground he was laughing so hard.

And I let him.

Whatever he needed to believe to keep my mate safe.

"So, we're agreed?"

"Yes. We're agreed."

That was great. But how was I going to make sure Trevor followed through with his deal?

"Does anyone have a phone, so I can let my elders know the deal's done? Then I'm all yours."

One of the younger kids was pushed forward and he timidly offered me a cell.

Again, strangest scene, ever.

I punched in the numbers for Sam's cell. He never answered his phone.

His voicemail kicked in and I cleared my throat, now strangely tight.

"Sam, it's Tayte. The bears have agreed to my terms and will take me in exchange for Celeste. They've also agreed to leave the pack alone, and everyone is to get on with their lives."

I hesitated to say more while the bears still listened.

"So, you take care. Thanks."

I hung up and my heart dropped, aching and bare.

Trevor clapped a hand over my shoulder.

"I have to say, wolf, you've got balls. I'll give you that."

They herded me out of the room, and I went willingly.

"Well, you know. Anything for the family, right?" I looked at him, Alpha to Alpha and expected to see some sort of camaraderie.

But instead, he looked away, then pushed me out the back door.

Into a fenced-in backyard filled with men and women and children.

"Welcome to your execution, wolf."

FOURTEEN

"That fucking idiot!"

I trembled with rage as Dane and I awaited the arrival of the cavalry. Dexter and Grayson and every other Alpha and Beta wolf in the pack were on their way.

We needed help taking down these bears and rescuing our Alpha.

We couldn't do it on our own.

And so I trembled with fear, a block away from the bear's apartment block.

"What now?" Dane demanded, pacing the sidewalk and cussing as he went back and forth.

I hung up the phone after I listened to the voice mail.

"Tayte. He's..." I swallowed. I knew he'd done it.

Before I'd gotten the confirmation, I knew he'd gone to the bears and offered himself up. But to hear it on my cell was a whole other level of grief.

I cleared my throat. "He's made a deal with the bears. His life for Celeste's, and peace between the two packs."

"He fucking what?" Dane glared at me.

I glared back. "What the hell are you looking at me like that for?"

"This is your fault! You blamed him for what happened to Celeste."

"So did you!" We all had, Claire included.

"I didn't want him to fucking die, though!" Dane's voice cut out halfway through his words.

I swallowed the lump in my throat as I struggled to hold back a wave of grief.

"I know... I know. Neither did I. I was just angry."

Angry that Fate had dealt us such an ugly hand. At Tayte, for being stupid enough to lie about the most important thing in our lives. And Celeste, for believing what she'd heard and not coming to us to find out if it was true.

I groaned as the realization hit.

I was angry at Celeste.

But I hadn't been able to feel that part of it. After what had happened to her that night, I'd pushed the anger down.

But part of me felt betrayed.

Betrayed that she'd snuck out to follow Tayte like he was doing something wrong. Betrayed that she'd run from us the first chance she got. Betrayed that she'd believed such an obvious and stupid lie.

After everything we'd said and done for her, that one lie was what she'd believed? So much so, that she'd endangered her own life and that of our daughter. And now, her disbelief had endangered Tayte's life, too.

I focused back on Dane as the screech and rumble of the pack's trucks pulled up and caught my attention.

"First thing's first. We have to save our Alpha before he becomes bear meat."

The procession of cars and trucks filled up the whole street.

The pack was here.

Dex jogged straight to me. "What's the situation?"

"Tayte's offered himself in exchange for Celeste and to stop any future attacks against the pack, so the bears have him and intend to kill him. They may have already done so."

I didn't think they'd be so quick about it, but what did I know about the execution strategies of bear shifters?

Dexter groaned. "This was not meant to happen. Tayte only said that stuff about Celeste to buy us some time to work out a better strategy than all-out war."

I glanced behind me, where dozens of young, healthy men were piling out of their cars.

"Well, it looks like the war is on."

Dexter nodded and went over to the rest of the pack members to explain what was going on.

"We need to go. Now." Dane nodded at a bunch of kids who'd spotted us.

They looked like bears, somehow, and when they began to run, we went after them.

We didn't want them alerting the adults to our presence.

"Dex! Gray!"

We ran, following the kids to a huge apartment block and straight through the front door of the place.

We could hear a ruckus in the backyard and charged down the corridor to where a horror story was unfolding before me.

Tayte was chained up against the fence, and it looked like they were taking turns beating him up. He was naked, bleeding and sliced.

"No!"

The shift came on me faster than it ever had.

I ran straight at the man with the knife, who was poised to stick it straight into Tayte's belly.

I clamped onto his wrist and ripped flesh from bone. Blood spurted through my teeth and I growled as I tore harder.

That's when the screaming began.

Women began to run, grabbing children, as my pack charged for the men.

Bear shifters began to shift and charge the wolves. The fight was on.

Whether we meant to begin a war or not, it seemed we were in one.

I stood in front of Tayte, growling and snapping at anyone who attempted to approach.

Then Dane's small, brown wolf bounded past me and shifted back to human.

"Oh, damn it, Tayte. What have you gone and done now?" Dane complained as he pulled at the bonds, managing to get Tayte off the fence.

I glanced at my Alpha. His arm was hanging at a weird angle. His gut was partially sliced open and as he fell forward and grabbed his belly, I almost vomited.

They'd actually gutted him, or tried to.

Part of his belly was spilling through his fingers.

I whirled around at the sound of vicious growling behind me.

A huge, black bear was down on all fours, charging me.

It was Trevor.

He was dead.

I ran straight at the bear, using the momentum to jump over him before twirling back and biting at his ears. His claws swung at my head.

I rolled and ducked and went for his hind legs.

Then there was another black wolf, flashing into my vision, coming to help me, and two huge silver wolves beside him.

It was us against them.

Two Alpha and two Beta wolves, taking down an Alpha bear.

I tore at his neck, sinking my teeth in and drawing blood.

This wasn't a fight where we'd just walk away after our point was made.

No. One side had to lose. Permanently.

And it couldn't be us.

Dexter's wolf tore at Trevor's eyes and face.

The other bears began to back away, not stepping up to support their Alpha but instead, running for their lives.

Some of our other wolves went after the bears that ran but I stayed and shifted back, my heart pounding in my chest as my human eyes took in the state of my Alpha.

He was on his knees with Dane beside him.

Oh, God.

They'd burnt his face and gashed his ear, too.

"We need to get you to the hospital. Let's go."

Dane and I put our arms around Tayte and he groaned in agony.

"My shoulder's... broken."

I tried to avoid touching his injuries, but it was almost impossible with the amount of wounds and blood on him.

"Your belly's more of a worry at the moment, Tayte. Let's go," I said.

I dragged my Alpha to our car and we rushed him to emergency.

At this rate we were going to need to build a hospital in our own town.

CHAPTER

FIFTEEN

DANE

My Alpha was in surgery, my mate was recovering from falling down a cliff and my daughter was in a humidicrib because she'd been born prematurely and by emergency C-section.

I put my head in my hands and closed my eyes.

"Things can't possibly get any worse," I muttered to Sam, as we sat in the horribly uncomfortable white chairs that lined the hospital waiting room. My stomach was in knots.

"I hope everyone else from the pack is okay."

Sam patted me on the shoulder. "Our pack is alive. Let's hold onto that. We'll find out about everyone else soon, I'm sure."

I stood up and stretched my back. "I'm going to see Celeste and the baby."

Sam nodded and ran his hand through his hair. "I'm gonna stay here and wait for the surgeons to come out and tell me about Tayte."

"Okay. Thanks, Sam."

I walked away from my Beta, my whole body feeling like it had been put on a torture rack and stretched.

What a day.

I pushed open the door to stop dead at the sight before me.

"She's out!" I said.

Celeste was breastfeeding our daughter, her beautiful flesh pressed against our daughter's bare skin.

Celeste looked up and beamed at me. "They said she's doing way better than they expected, and I finally got to hold her. To nurse her! Look how strong she is."

I walked up next to the bed and watched as the baby suckled strongly.

I kissed my mate's forehead, the warmth in the room making Celeste feel hot to the touch, even in the light gown she barely wore.

"You're amazing, she's amazing. Hey, have you thought of a name yet?"

She looked up at me, her blue eyes big and wide.

"I have, but I wanted to ask Tayte before I told anyone else. Where is he? Is he okay?"

Not really.

I grabbed a chair that leaned against the wall and pulled it over to sit closer to my mate.

I couldn't resist reaching out and stroking the baby's soft head. "She has blonde hair."

Celeste grabbed my wrist. "Dane, how's Tayte?"

I ran my hand through my hair. "He's um...."

"He's not dead. Tell me he's not dead." Her voice sounded panicked and I rushed to reassure her.

"He's not dead."

That was all I could tell her, though.

"Then where is he?"

"He's in surgery."

She swallowed, hard, her already pale skin going even more pale. "Why? I mean, what's the surgery for?"

I didn't really want to recall all the injuries my Alpha had sustained.

"Ah… dislocated shoulder, knife wound to the belly, burned face, cut off ear…"

Tears sprouted and slid down Celeste's face.

"Burned face… knife… oh my God."

I grabbed her hand and squeezed it.

"I suppose we have to be grateful the bears were taking their time killing him, or we may have arrived too late."

"I don't know what to say. Is he going to be okay?"

"I don't know."

She began to cry as she rocked the baby.

"Dane, I didn't want this to happen. Not like this. I mean, I was so angry at him, but now…"

I stroked her head and kissed her hair. "I know. It puts it all in perspective, doesn't it?"

She nodded. "Yes, it does."

The baby came off Celeste's nipple, her eyes closed and her mouth still open.

Milk dribbled down the side of her face.

"Do you want to hold her?"

I glanced down at her.

"I'd love to, but I'm not very clean."

I gestured down to my clothes that were some of the spares we kept in the car in case of emergencies.

"The doctors asked why Tayte was naked when we brought him in, but we didn't have much of an explanation."

Celeste put the baby over her shoulder and gently rubbed her back.

"So, what's going to happen? Do you know?"

I shook my head. "I have no idea. Wolf shifters have abnormal healing powers, which probably is one of the reasons the baby is doing better than they all expected. We're strong and fit and healthy, but Tayte's injuries were... extensive."

I swallowed hard against the lump in my throat.

"We can only wait, I suppose. Sam's sitting in the waiting room now."

Celeste nodded, then sobbed softly.

"I can't believe this all happened. Actually, I can. I always knew my baggage would haunt us, follow me. But I never thought... I hoped it would all be okay."

I could see the tide had turned and Celeste was going to start to blame herself now.

"Sweetheart, this isn't your fault. It's no one's fault, really. It's some, fucked-up twist of Fate. A lesson we needed to learn, a fire we had to walk through. I don't know. But the only thing I need to know is if you'll still love us when this is all settled?"

I stared at her, hoping, praying that these past few days hadn't changed her mind about us.

She gasped for air as though she'd been holding her breath.

"Of course, I still love you! Loving you all has never been a problem, but after I heard Tayte say what he said, I felt so betrayed! So hurt. I couldn't believe that after everything we'd been through..."

She stopped, gasping for air again and that's when I grabbed her hands and made her look at me.

"That's exactly where you should have stopped, turned around, and demanded an answer from Tayte. And if not from him, then me or Sam. You can't just run away at the first hurdle, Celeste. That's not what this relationship is about. There's three of us to check on, and you can't run because one of us pisses you off. That's not fair to anyone."

Celeste nodded and gulped.

I grabbed a glass of water and handed it to her.

"Yes. I know," she said, once she'd taken a few sips from the glass.

"Good. Because we adore you. Every single, tiny part of you."

She nodded and swallowed some more water.

I sighed, utterly exhausted.

I hadn't slept properly in two days, and I couldn't even reach out to my daughter because there was blood on my hands.

Quite literally.

"Excuse me while I go wash up a bit in your bathroom."

I opened the door and ran water into the sink, wiping at my face, my hands, my arms.

"What happened with the bears? You didn't tell me."

I ducked my face under the water and washed away the grime of the morning.

Then I patted myself dry with one of those small, white hospital towels, then threw it on the floor, in the corner.

Sorry to the staff member who had to launder that one.

"Um..." I walked back into the room to watch Celeste swaddling up the baby, then holding her while she slept. "I don't know, completely. We were winning when I left. But I needed to get Tayte to the hospital, so we'll have to wait to find out from one of the other Alphas. Hopefully there weren't many casualties on our side."

She nodded, then put the baby into the crib beside her bed.

"Okay, but will they still be after us? Is Trevor..."

"Oh, no." I kept forgetting she wasn't there. "We killed Trevor. He's gone. And a lot of the male bear shifters, too."

Celeste's eyes widened again and her skin turned even more pale.

"Well, that's... great. I suppose."

"Are you okay?"

I understood that she'd be feeling a combination of happiness and sorrow. After all, they had been her family for a very long time.

"Yes, I just... never thought I'd be happy that someone was dead."

I almost laughed. But thought I might get slapped if I did.

Instead, I sat next to my mate and held her hand.

"I get that."

"So, what do we do now?"

"We wait."

CHAPTER

SIXTEEN

TAYTE

Damn, my head hurt.

I forced my eyes to open, though they didn't want to. There was Sam, by my side. In a stark white room I had to assume was the hospital.

"Hey." I swallowed, trying to make my mouth work properly. I was as dry as the desert.

"Hey, yourself," Sam said, standing up. "How are you feeling?"

"Like I got pulled through a hedge—backwards."

Everything hurt. My head, my chest, my belly, my legs.

"Yeah, well you did a pretty good job of almost dying, but we weren't gonna let you."

"How? Oh..."

The memories of this morning came back to me in a flash of pain and knives and cruel laughter. "The bears."

"Yes, the bears. What were you thinking, giving yourself over to them?"

He sounded angry at me, which was strange. After everything that had happened with Celeste, I'd thought Sam would be relieved to get rid of me.

"I was fixing all our problems in one go. The bears would leave the pack alone, and you three could be happy without me."

That got me a soft punch in the arm.

"Ow."

My head spun from the pain and he shoved a handle into my palm.

"Push this button. It's morphine."

I glanced down at the green button and pressed it. Anything to help with the throb in my brain.

"Thanks."

I lay my head back and tried to swallow again. It was like the desert in my mouth.

"Is there any water?"

Sam handed me a cup and I swallowed some down, the brief wetness enough to get my tongue to unstick from the roof of my mouth.

I closed my eyes, the pain dragging on me.

"How's Celeste? Is she okay?"

There was silence in response to my question and then the whoosh of a curtain.

"How 'bout you ask her yourself?"

I lifted my head and opened my eyes.

There was my beautiful mate, standing in the doorway. Her hair fell around her like a halo, and she held our baby in her arms.

Tears filled her eyes as she stared at me.

I tried to smile, unsure of the response I'd get from her. I was pretty sure last time we'd spoken, she'd broken up with me. "Hey, beautiful."

Celeste sobbed as she threw herself down on to the bed with me. I suppressed my groan of pain as she placed her head on my chest, the baby cradled between us.

"Tayte... oh my God. You're okay."

She lifted her face to me, her eyes shiny with the unshed tears.

She'd forgiven me?

I tentatively reached down with my good hand and cupped her face.

"Of course, I'm okay. How are you?"

She sobbed again and pushed herself up so that she could kiss my lips, the saltiness of her tears on my tongue.

When she pulled back, my heart ached. I'd missed her love so much.

She sniffed and wiped at her face. "I was so worried about you. I am so sorry about what happened the other night. I should never have even been there, let alone believed the lies you told the bears. I should have known better, and I am so, so, sorry for everything."

Tears fell down her face and I looked to Sam for guidance.

He just sat in the chair, watching and waiting.

I rubbed her back with my good arm, then pulled it back in close to me, the pain too great to move far.

"Stop crying, Celeste, it's okay. I totally understand why you wanted me to move out. It's your right to reject any one of us, if you have cause. And you did. But I couldn't stand by while my pack and the whole town was in danger. I saw a way out, for all of us. So I took it."

Celeste hoisted up the baby and placed her on my chest on her stomach.

She was the most perfect little thing. Rosebud lips and pale, soft skin.

I would have missed all of this.

Celeste shook her head. "No. You should have stayed and fought to remain in our family. This little girl needs her daddy, and I don't want you to ever, no matter what, think of leaving us again. I promise you, it will be the same for me. No more running away."

I looked at my mate, and then back to my daughter, my eyes burning with the strangest feeling.

I swallowed hard. Did this mean that everything was okay? That they still wanted me?

"What have you called her?"

Celeste smiled and stroked the baby's head.

"I haven't named her anything yet. I wanted your approval."

I raised my good arm to touch my baby's soft hair.

"All right. What would you like to call her?"

Celeste met my gaze and I saw a lot of love and uncertainty there. "Destiny. After all, it was Destiny that brought us together."

I smiled as the sound of our daughter's name rolled around the room.

"Sounds perfect to me. Contingent on the rest of the family's approval, of course."

I glanced at my Beta and Omega, both of whom nodded happily.

"We're happy with anything you choose."

"Destiny, then."

I lifted my daughter up higher on my chest and kissed the top of her head.

Celeste leaned close and rested her cheek against my shoulder.

I had to ask—my head was whirling with all the uncertainties left.

"So, we're okay? After I get better, I can come home?"

I never thought I'd have to ask my pack such a thing, and Sam's eyes were shadowed as he stared at me.

"It's only a home with you in it, Tayte. You're the foundation of everything in our family."

I blinked away the tears that gathered in my eyes once again and put it down to all the drugs in my system.

I let my body relax into the pillows and looked at my family.

They weren't going anywhere, and thanks to a stroke of luck, now... neither was I.

EPILOGUE

CELESTE

A year later

I looked down at the white stick and smiled as my stomach flipped over.

Two pink lines. Clear and visible.

I was pregnant.

Again.

"Oh."

We'd celebrated Destiny's first birthday only yesterday, and I'd been feeling a little queasy all day.

I'd had my suspicions, of course, but I'd wanted to wait until after the party to do an official test.

Unlike that day, all those months ago when I found out I was pregnant the first time, this day would be cause for celebration, not despair.

What a difference a year and a half made.

I slid the cap back on the test stick and placed it into my back pocket. The men were out, but they'd be home for lunch soon.

"How you going, baby girl? You ready to get changed?"

Destiny was sitting in her highchair, having inhaled a banana, a sandwich and some berries.

She ate more than I did.

I glanced at the clock and counted. I had about ten minutes before my triad arrived home.

"Let's go, beautiful girl."

I picked up my daughter and carried her to the nursery, cleaning the crumbs and berry smudges off her angelic face.

I squealed a little as I opened the new t-shirt and changed her into the outfit that I'd ordered online. It had arrived last week and was a perfect fit for my daughter.

I stood her up and she teetered a little.

Her t-shirt read, "*I'm going to be a big sister.*"

"Perfect."

Destiny toddled over to the corner of her room and began to play.

What a year it had been!

Tayte had spent months recovering from his injuries and surgeries. The wolf genes helped his healing tremendously, but it still took a long time before everything was well again.

Both with him, and with us.

But every day we'd worked on rebuilding the trust again.

Every day I loved them all that little bit more.

So much so, that now, if I heard them tell anyone I wasn't their fated mate, or they'd get rid of me to save the pack, I'd laugh in their face.

My men lived and breathed our family.

They loved me and my daughter, and since the moment I put Destiny on Tayte's chest, I hadn't looked back.

Not at that night I thought they wanted to get rid of me. Not to my horrible childhood or the months before I met Tayte.

My life was blessed.

I was Cinderella in my fairy tale, and I had three Prince Charmings to love, and who loved me back. Every single day.

"Celeste!"

My heart leapt as they entered the house—loudly—as they always did.

"Daddy!" Destiny called out as she stumbled, trying to run past me. She got a few more steps into the living room before she fell to the floor and cried as she always did.

Tayte laughed as he scooped her up and showered her with kisses.

"How's my perfect girl? Have you been good for Mommy?"

Sam came for me first, which was nice, and gave me a swift kiss. "Are you okay? You looked a little pale this morning."

I nodded. "I'm great. How was work?"

"Busy."

Dane came in and shut the door, grabbing for Destiny and whirling her around.

"Something smells good. What's for lunch?" he asked.

None of them had noticed Destiny's top yet and my stomach was in knots, waiting for them to discover the surprise.

Of course, I assumed they'd be happy about the new pregnancy. After all, they put in daily efforts to make sure I was constantly filled with their desire for me.

But it didn't stop the anxiety that rattled through me.

"Um... lamb curry. I wanted to try a new recipe."

"Great. I'm starving."

The men all piled into the kitchen and I started serving them, putting lots of rice in every bowl as I knew how many calories they burned through in a day.

"Hey, Celeste?" There was a strange note in Dane's voice.

"Yeah?" I asked as I put each bowl down in front of my men.

Dane was looking at me with a huge smile on his face. "What does this mean?"

He pointed to Destiny's top, where she stood on his thigh and clung to his neck.

He turned her around and showed the other two men, who went silent.

My heart leapt in my chest and I swallowed quickly, my hand trembling as I pulled out the stick from my back pocket.

"Well... I'm pregnant."

The three men looked at one another for a single second, then jumped to their feet, whooping loudly.

"That's brilliant!"

Sam grabbed me and kissed me, then Tayte picked me up and twirled me around.

"How are you feeling?"

I put my hand out to steady myself. "A little woozy, but happy. Are you three happy, too?"

Dane kissed me soundly, still holding Destiny, then wrapped his arm around my shoulders.

"We couldn't be happier. More babies for our family, and a baby brother or sister for our perfect girl."

He nuzzled his nose against Destiny's face, who cackled and wriggled to get down.

Dane put her on the ground and she toddled off to her room.

My triad surrounded me, holding me in that long, intense way they had, that always made me feel loved.

"I love you. All of you," I said. "Thank you for my new life."

Tayte swung me into his arms and carried me up the stairs.

"Lunch can wait. I think we need to celebrate now."

Dane stayed with Destiny and Sam followed us into our main bedroom.

They'd swap after a while, and if I passed out from exhaustion, one of them would call into work and tell them they were taking the afternoon off.

My life truly was perfect.

I had my men, my child and a village of people who loved and supported us.

It seriously couldn't get any better than this.

THE END

~

I hope you've loved reading about the Woodland Wolf packs!
Reverse Harem and wolf shifters make the perfect pairing!
Which is why I wrote- Halloween Witches. Another wolf shifter
reverse harem series.

If you've enjoyed this series, you will love Alpha Magic.

You can download and read it:
https://books2read.com/u/38dG5r
Or read on for a sneak peek into book 1.

~

PROLOGUE

Halloween night. One year ago.

Our mothers said that three of us were Fated, blessed. What she meant was, I would be stuck with these two pain-in-the-ass best friends until my dying day.

"So, are we going to do this, or not?" I asked my friends, staring at each of them in turn. "Because there's no going back after this."

My heart was pounding like a runaway train and if we didn't cast the spell now, I was afraid we'd never have the guts to do it.

The wind moved through the trees around us, rustling the leaves and signaling a Fall storm was on its way. We were gathered outside beneath the full moon and dark, starless sky, on a large piece of property in the middle of nowhere.

No one could see us, and as long as we never said a word, nobody would ever know about our little adventure on this night.

This Halloween night. Our joint twenty-first birthday.

Tiffany, the blonde bombshell of our little group, nodded fiercely. I could see the determination in her bright blue eyes. She wanted this as much I did.

I turned to Bella, who had her teeth buried firmly in her lower lip.

I rolled my eyes. "Come on, Bella. You know we can't do this without you."

And I meant that literally. Bella was a powerful witch and without her magic, I wasn't sure Tiff and I could pull off a spell of this magnitude.

She frowned and I could see the hesitation in the set of her shoulders, in her dark brown gaze.

I narrowed my eyes at the girl who'd been practically a sister to me since the day we'd been born. "Come on, Bella. Please."

We'd been talking about this spell for years, planning every part of the complex incantation. Waiting until the night we were old enough... powerful enough... gutsy enough, to pull it off.

Suddenly Bella's gaze hardened, and relief poured through me. I knew that look. She was on my side now.

"Okay, Ruby. I'm in. Let's do this."

I grabbed my two best friends' hands and they grabbed each other, forming a perfect triangle of strength.

We were three witches born on the same day, the most powerful day of the year for our kind. All Hallows' Eve.

Our mothers were best friends, united in the abandonment by the fathers of their children. They'd made sure we grew up together, strong, bonded, and most of all, loyal to one another.

We clasped hands and glanced down at the book between us, a spell book I'd found ten years ago, hidden in my mother's things. A powerful spell book that had belonged to my late grandmother.

We began to chant in an ancient language that no one used anymore.

I closed my eyes, having memorized the spell years ago. I spoke my part and my friends spoke theirs. Each section was a call to the magic that rippled in our veins. To Fate. And most of all, to the unconditional love that we all desired and craved.

Over and over we chanted our words, the magic in our blood, in our ancestry, simmering and bursting at the seams.

I could feel the heat in my body building until sweat rolled down my face. I didn't stop, and neither did Bella or Tiffany. The power of our combined words swirled around us like a hurricane, and I clung to the spell, focusing everything I had on this night. This one moment, where we would make sure that we'd never end up like our mothers, abandoned and alone.

My eyes opened. The ancient book floated in the air between us. Bella was watching the book with trepidation and Tiff grinned when she caught my eye.

We began to speak louder, the words in our hearts building naturally as the spell came to a crescendo. I stared at our joined hands as white light built between our clenched fingers.

There was a sudden surge of power, and the urge to finish the spell gripped me. I nodded at my honorary sisters and together we spoke the last of our parts. There was no going back now.

As we uttered those last few words, the white magic we'd conjured shot into the air above our heads, exploding into a spectacular spray of fireworks highlighted against the dark night sky.

The impact of the explosion blew us back and apart, each of us landing with a thump on the grass.

I groaned as I rolled onto my side to take pressure off the bruised parts of my backside but I didn't look away from the sky as the magic exploded, then seemed to disappear.

A small amount of disappointment hit me. I'd expected more than some white fireworks, then dissipation. Though what I'd thought would happen, I didn't know.

As we sat on the ground surrounded by nature and trees and the gorgeous country house off in the distance, peace stole over me.

"Is that it?" I asked, and as though in answer, the spell book that had been hovering in the air between us, landed in the dirt. The front cover closed, all signs of magic, gone.

Tiffany stood first, brushing the dirt from her tight pants and groaning as though annoyed by the mess.

Bella and I got to our feet too, the excitement and build-up to this day beginning to leach the strength out of me.

It was over. It was done. Now, all we had to do was wait for the spell to come to fruition. For the men—our men—to come to us.

And patience, although I'd been told was a virtue, was not one of my strengths.

"So... back to the house for a celebratory drink?" I suggested, forcing some excitement into my tone.

We'd brought some alcohol with us. Why wouldn't we, when we could finally legally drink in the human world?

"Sounds like a plan," Tiffany said with a flick of her long hair, and together we turned and trekked back to the house that Bella's family owned.

I glanced down at my hands, expecting something to have

changed. But as I glanced at each of my friends, it seemed that nothing was different for any of us. Not physically, anyway.

I wondered if our loves, wherever they were, had been hit with our magic. Could they feel it, even now? Were they searching for us?

Once inside the little house in the woods, we flicked on the lights and used our magic to mix up cocktails the color of the sunset—red, yellow, and a splash of purple.

"Perfect." I picked up my glass that had been resting on the counter.

Tiffany and Bella plucked up their drinks as well, raising their glasses to clink with mine.

"Happy birthday," I said, and they chorused back to me.

Sharing a birthday with my two best friends had been trying at times, especially growing up. I'd never had my own party, or a single day when I could feel simply special just for being me.

But now, I loved it.

We all took a sip of our first legal drink and grimaced at the amount of liquor I'd poured in.

"Wow, that's strong," Tiff said, blinking rapidly.

I nodded, swallowing hard as the vodka and gin mix slid down my throat.

Bella gulped awkwardly, shuddering before she set the drink back down on the counter. She waved her hand over the table in front of us and conjured up a whole feast of savory and sweet snacks. Chips, chocolate cake, cookies, and crackers with cheese littered the surface in front of us.

She was the best at making food. Actually, she was the best of everything when it came to magic. But luckily for us, as the most introverted of our trio, she never threw it in our faces.

"Oh, perfect. Thanks, Belle."

I grabbed some chips and stuffed them in my mouth. I hadn't eaten dinner with all the nerves surrounding tonight.

Bella sighed and I glanced up at her, raising my eyebrows in question. It was obvious she wanted to ask me something.

"What's up Bell-Bell?"

"Do you think it worked?" she asked, speaking aloud the question we all wanted answered.

I shrugged, forcing myself to appear nonchalant, though I was anything but. This spell would hopefully change the course of all our lives for the better.

I gave her the only answer I could. "I don't know. I hope so."

"So do I!" Tiffany said, her tone exasperated. "We've only been planning this forever."

I conjured up some stools and we all sat down around our little birthday feast.

We chatted and ate, drank and laughed, celebrating our whole lives ahead of us.

Through the night I hoped that our magic was working its way to the men for whom we were destined, because the spell we had woven together tonight was a spell that called out to destiny. For our one, true love.

All three of our mothers had been abandoned before we were even born. We'd grown up around sorrow and loneliness. Heartache.

None of us wanted that for ourselves or any future children we might have.

So tonight, we'd sent out a call for the men who would love us for all eternity. Our perfect matches. Men who would stand by us. Love us. Never leave us.

We wanted them quickly of course, but they would answer the call when they were good and ready. Or at least, that was what I assumed.

Whether that be tomorrow, next month, or next year, I would wait. And I knew Bella and Tiffany would, too.

Because only Fate could be trusted with such an important a decision as the person we were meant to spend the rest of our lives with.

Born to three single mothers, not a father between us, we had trust issues aplenty. I, for one, wasn't going to just date anyone.

And I certainly wasn't going to fall in love with the first guy who happened to look my way. I'd rather be alone forever than live with the pain my mother wore like a heavy coat.

So hopefully, Fate and our own magic would not let us down, because we'd risked everything tonight to make our futures happen.

ONE

One year later.

My day job at the local florist certainly wasn't glamorous, but it passed the time all the same.

"Have a nice day," I said to the human woman who'd bought a bunch of roses for her sick mother. I waved her out the door. What I really should have done was tuck in a spell for her mother's flu, but we weren't allowed to do magic around the humans in town.

I let out a huge sigh and looked around the large shop filled with buckets of brightly colored flowers and potted plants. What was I doing here again?

Making yourself useful until you work out what you want to do with your life, my mother's voice sounded in my head.

The witches in my family were healers, fortune tellers, teachers. But unlike all those women who had come before me, I had no idea what I wanted to do with my life at this point.

I'd graduated high school with good grades, gone to community college, then... nothing.

I was adrift, and that wasn't my personality generally. I wasn't a flake. But unlike so many of the witching community who were addicted to the coven lifestyle, I just... wasn't.

I wasn't even sure if I wanted to hang around this town forever. Travel sounded more interesting to me, seeing the world. If only I could convince Bella and Tiffany to come.

"Ruby, I'm just heading to the bank. Do you want me to grab anything for your lunch?" Andrea, my boss, smiled at me as she picked up her handbag from behind the counter and headed to the front door.

"No. I'm all good today. Thanks, Andrea." I waved at her as she left.

Such a lovely woman, especially for a human.

When my mother had realized I couldn't make up my mind on what I wanted to do with my life, she'd forced me to get a job with a non-magical person. To learn, to expand my horizons. To be "of use to the community".

Which, at the time, I'd thought was a horrible idea. But as it turned out, there were a lot of nice humans here.

The school I'd attended had been mostly for witches, and I'd kept my head down at college and mostly associated with those I knew. Again, mostly witches.

Now, it was kind of nice to be able to weave between the different communities, not that the humans knew what I was, of course.

I turned back to the flowers I'd been arranging when my last customer had come in. A phone order had come through for a large bunch of lilies and violets. Simple, but lovely.

I was so tempted to use my magic to make them bright, bigger, more beautiful. But there were severe consequences for revealing magic to the non-magicals.

So, instead, I practiced my hand skills. I arranged them in a nice bunch, wrapping paper and plastic around the stems, then tying it off with an orange ribbon to contrast the vivid purple color of the violets.

The bell above the door tinkled as a new customer pushed it open.

"With you in a moment," I called over my shoulder toward the front door, and a tingle of awareness shot up my spine.

I shivered, not with cold but with impending change. My breath caught in my throat as I twisted around to see who had set off such a drastic shift in the world around me.

A huge man stood in the shop, staring at me with quiet intensity.

His rugged beauty struck me like a slap to the face. Soulful, dark blue eyes. Brown hair falling to his shoulders. Features so stunning it made me want to crawl over the counter and jump into his arms.

The only thing that stopped me from doing exactly that was the fact that the person standing before me staring at me like he'd never seen a woman before, wasn't just a man. I took a deep breath through my nose and shivered at the gruff, animalistic notes.

He was so much more than just a shifter. He was a wolf. Not just any wolf, an Alpha.

I'd come across one once by accident when I was a child in the forest. The scent of an Alpha was like barely leashed power, earthy sweat and strong animal. I'd never forgotten how I'd felt that day, and now I was standing before another one. This time, in human form.

I placed my hands on the counter in front of me, digging my nails into the wood so that I didn't squeal or scream or any of those immensely embarrassing female reactions that finding your one true love was bound to bring out in even the calmest of women.

I cleared my throat with a cough and forced myself to look up at him. "Can I help you?"

He had the brightest, sharpest blue eyes. The darkest hair. And if he wasn't six feet six, I'd bite my own bum.

"You're a witch," he said, no inflection in his voice indicating it was a question.

"Shh..." I said, hushing him. "You're lucky my boss has gone to the bank."

He frowned. "She doesn't know?"

"We don't tell humans what we are. You know that." I crossed my arms over my chest and raised an eyebrow at him. "Do you go around shouting to the humans that you're an Alpha wolf shifter?"

His eyes went wide, and he stared at me with his mouth open. He looked as if I'd hit him over the head with a frying pan.

"What's wrong? Cat got your tongue?" I asked, grinning at him for long moments.

Damn, he's beautiful. So beautiful.

Though that was probably the wrong word for his appearance. His jaw was darkened with the beginnings of a new beard and the muscles bulging under the gray hoodie he wore hinted at an incredibly lethal body.

Hot... he was damn HOT.

"What are you?" he asked, almost as an accusation.

"What do you mean, what am I?" I repeated and frowned at him. He knew I was a witch. What more did he want? "I'm Ruby. Why? What's wrong?"

"How did you know that about me?" he asked. "I'm not the Alpha... not yet, anyway."

"But it's in your blood, isn't it?" I asked, second-guessing myself now. I couldn't be wrong about that, could I? The other Alpha I'd met was in wolf form.

He took a few steps forward, his intense blue gaze staying focused on me. "Yes, it is. So, answer my question. How'd you know that?"

My breath caught in my throat the closer he moved, the scent of him so familiar, like a long-forgotten memory. But how was that possible? I'd never met him before. I was sure of it.

"I..." I swallowed and dropped my arms, grabbing for the counter again as my knees threatened to buckle beneath me. "I met an Alpha wolf when I was child. He smelled the same as you."

The Alpha crept closer until he stood right in front of the counter I was leaning on for support.

I had to tilt my head up to look into his eyes, and when I did, a noise came out of my mouth that I couldn't decipher.

A moan? A prayer? A curse?

What is this?

I gripped the counter as my trembling legs finally gave way. This was going to hurt if I didn't save myself.

I muttered a spell word and conjured a chair beneath me. I fell into it, feeling as intoxicated as I assumed drunk felt.

Witches had a great resistance to alcohol, like most paranormals, so I'd never felt what being tipsy was like, let alone been fully intoxicated. But I had to assume it felt like this strange, hot, tingly feeling that pulsed through my veins, making me weak, weepy, and strangely aroused.

Damn, that's what this is! Arousal. Heat pulsated from my core, radiating through my belly and down my legs.

I forced myself to look up at him, and he was staring at me as though he were waiting for something. "Um..." My brain had gone all stupid and blank. "Did you ask me another question?"

He shook his head and growled a little, swallowing and coughing as though he suddenly couldn't speak.

What was going on?

The bell tinkled again over the front door and Andrea strolled back in.

I jumped to my feet and made my chair disappear before she saw it.

"Welcome back," I greeted her, putting on my cheeriest smile and happiest voice, though inside my head, my world was spinning.

This guy... this wolf shifter... he had to be my soul mate. The one I'd called for on Halloween last year. Didn't he? Nothing else made sense.

He was so much hotter, bigger... older than I'd imagined.

But I'd never expected a wolf shifter. *Damn.* How was my mom gonna take this news?

Andrea placed her black handbag on the counter and frowned at the Alpha wolf in front of me. "Can I help you?"

I was surprised by her non-welcoming response, especially for one of the friendliest women I'd ever met. Didn't she feel his strength, his power? How wasn't she affected by his beauty?

Then something my mother had once told me swam up into my subconscious. *Humans don't like shifters.* Wolves, especially. They could feel the danger in them, which to us, was an aphrodisiac. However, for a human, it only smelled like trouble.

And boy, am I in trouble...

The guy nodded at Andrea and pushed a piece of paper across the desk at us.

I glanced down at it. An order of lilies and violets.

"Oh, these are for you, sir!" I squawked in my nervousness to diffuse the situation. I didn't want Andrea to be angry at him. He wasn't doing anything wrong.

I twisted around, grabbed the flowers I'd just been arranging, and turned back to him in a hurry. I leaned over the counter and offered them to the huge man I was pretty certain was meant to be mine.

"Thank you," he managed to say, though he sounded garbled and his teeth were unusually pointed as he forced the words out.

Almost... wolf-like. His teeth hadn't looked like that when he'd come into the shop.

He pulled out a credit card from his wallet and I glanced down at the name before sliding it through the sensor on the side of the register monitor. I couldn't help myself.

Jackson Davis.

Oh, I liked the sound of that. But where did he live? Where was he from? Was he just passing through town or did he belong to a pack in the area?

I have to find out!

I processed his payment and handed back the plastic.

He plucked the card from my hand with his fingertips, careful not to touch me as he took it. A flush of disappointment washed over me. I ached to touch him, to see if I could feel something tangible and physical between us.

I was early in my training as a witch, but all my teachers said I had a natural affinity for scrying. Future predictions. And my instincts were always on target.

And every instinct, every vibe, every ounce of my witchy genes, was telling me that Jackson and I would be seeing *a lot* more of each other in the future.

"Thank you," he mumbled again as he backed away, though he barely opened his mouth to speak this time.

I cocked my head at him and watched as he began to retreat. What was with the talking thing? Or more precisely, the lack of talking thing?

Was he fighting the urge to shift? Did he feel the attraction between us that radiated like the sun? I wanted to know so badly what was going on inside his head.

"Oh, ah..." I tried to call out to him as he left, but he practically ran for the door, the bells clanging as he threw himself outside.

I stared at him through the window as he hopped into his truck and squealed out of his parking spot in front of the shop before I even had time to walk around the counter.

Andrea shook her head and *tsked* loudly as she opened the cash register and began unloading the change she'd gotten from the bank. "He sounded like such a nice man on the phone. I'm sorry you had to wait on him while I was out. I'm sure he scared you."

"Scared me?" I repeated, moving away from Andrea to arrange some nearby roses. Idle hands... devil's work, and all that.

"Oh, yes," Andrea said, shuddering. "Didn't he bother you? The size of him... the feel of him. Ugh." She shuddered again.

I clenched my jaw. Why didn't she understand that there was nothing wrong with him but instead, something wrong with her?

But I swallowed down my anger. It was for the good of the humans that they were afraid of the shifters. It was natural. And I shouldn't be offended.

Even though my face was flushed with heat, and rage bubbled inside me.

It's a good thing. It's a good thing. Don't get mad.

I faced the roses I was toying with so she couldn't see my red face and forced myself to continue with normal conversation. "Who were the flowers for? His wife? Did he say?"

There hadn't been a card ordered so I was left hoping someone hadn't snagged him before I could.

"His grandmother, I think," Andrea said as she went into the back to check stock and I was left staring out the window.

Was this the man I was meant to love? The one that our Halloween spell had called upon? Everything in me said yes.

But none of us three, not Tiffany, not Bella, not me, had even had a single date since that fateful night exactly twelve months ago.

But from the feel of Jackson Davis and the prickling of the hairs at the nape of my neck, I was pretty sure I'd just met my one. My only. My soulmate.

And he was a wolf shifter.

Damn. I hope the coven doesn't mind!

www.ingramcontent.com/pod-product-compliance
Lightning Source LLC
Chambersburg PA
CBHW070957190726
48292CB00004B/1489